MW01127590

Wander

By

Orlando A. Sanchez

A Night Warden Novel

The world is a playground, and death is the night.-Rumi

This one is for you Mom.

Who, like Grey, wandered alone most of her life. Your love of reading planted the seed to allow me to chase the dream of writing. Your strength, perseverance, and wicked sense of humor showed me how to make it real.

I love you.

Published by Bitten Peaches Publishing NY NY

Cover Design by Gene Mollica Studios. LLC.
www.genemollica.com

ONE

I HEARD THE scream first.

Frankly I was prepared to keep walking. Out here this late, in this neighborhood, you reap what you sow. The night culls the weak and the foolish. Then she begged for her life. It was a small voice, desperate, and clinging to a false hope. She was looking for mercy where none existed.

Cruel laughter was the answer to her pleas.

"Shit," I said as I turned towards the dead-end street. A bitterness filled my mouth as I shook my head. Ambient magic caused my taste buds to fire one of the side effects of my condition.

An ogre, the source of the foul taste, closed in on the woman. It was a large man-shaped creature. Scars covered its muscular body and their faces were not recommended viewing before any meal.

I saw her then. She was dressed in a simple dress and looked to be some kind of server on her way home from her shift. She had to be mid-twenties. Too young to know better, too old to admit it. Next to the ogre, I saw the rummer—a pseudo vamp, user of Redrum. At the opening of the street stood a man, watching. He wore a black uniform, which was a cross between combat armor and formal wear. The two creatures would drain her dry, right after the ogre ripped off an arm or two.

"As I live and breathe, Grey Stryder, washed up, partner killer coming to grace me with his presence," the man said when he saw me. "You need to leave, old man, while you still can."

"Always a pleasure to see you, Alex, like smashing my hand in a car door, goddamn unforgettable and excruciating."

"What the hell is this look? Homeless senior citizen?"

I ran a hand through my buzz cut. There was a time I'd be wearing the same uniform. On the streets freshly shaven and ready for patrol. Those days were long gone.

"What brings you to my neighborhood?"

"Back the hell off, " Alex said and I saw his fingers start to move. "This is Night Warden business and I don't need a retired Warden dinosaur interfering."

"Night Warden business?" I asked, opening my duster and glancing down the street. "Since when does Night Warden business include whatever this is?"

"Since you just put the *dead* in dead-end, and turned down the wrong street."

He gestured, black energy covering his hands. I drew my gun, Fatebringer and fired. He died on the way to the ground.

"I never retired, you piece of sh—"

Another scream. I turned into the street.

"Nice night," I whispered, knowing they could hear me. "She seems small for the two of you. Not much meat on her. Maybe leave her to the ogre? The woman's red-rimmed eyes opened wider at my words. She was cowering next to a dumpster. She tried to make herself smaller as the large creature lumbered in her direction.

I had trouble determining which was worse—the odor from the dumpster or the odor from the ogre. As I closed in, the aroma from the ogre wrapped itself around me, squeezed my lungs and brought tears to my eyes. Old garbage would be refreshing after that.

The ogre ignored me, focused on the meal in front of it. The rummer snapped his neck around, hissing in my direction. Redrum destroys most of the brain, turning the rummers into little more than ravenous animals incapable of speech. It didn't mean they were harmless. They were faster, stronger, and more resilient than normals.

The drug gave them heightened senses, night vision, enhanced hearing, and an insane sense of smell. A mindless, deadly package. Another drawback—a few minutes of UV radiation led to an explosive messy end.

I dodged the first swipe. Razor-sharp claws raked the air where my head had been a moment earlier. I kicked out and sent the rummer flying—right into the ogre.

The ogre turned and faced me.

"I'm going to kill you, little wizard," it said, as it lumbered in my direction, forgetting the woman.

Some mages get touchy about the whole mage-wizard thing. Me? I couldn't care less. My casting days were long behind me, even if my body still gave off a runic signature.

I fired Fatebringer, which I loaded with LIT rounds. Light Irradiated Tungsten—vampire killers—were perfect rummer erasers, but they were useless against the mountain of hate coming my way. I fired anyway. I made sure to put some distance between the woman and us. I hoped she would take the hint and bolt. One glance her way told me she had entered designated victim mode, crouching farther into a corner.

The rummer flanked me and lunged. I rolled, landing on my back, and fired twice. The rummer looked down at the wound and growled at me. It should have exploded into little rummer bits. It didn't. It crawled along the floor and leaped. I put two more rounds in it mid-leap. It kept coming. Those claws were looking sharp as it closed the distance. I dodged to the side and avoided another rake. It hissed at me and crouched for another attack.

Two seconds later, the rummer exploded all over my coat. I wiped the ichor from my eyes just in time to see the ogre shuffle forward, bury a fist in my side, and send me skidding across the ground. I rolled to my feet, took a deep breath, and switched magazines.

Entropy rounds were considered illegal and banned munitions. I considered them essential. The first round barely slowed the ogre down. I slid to the side and fired twice more. The ogre introduced me to a backhand that nearly broke my jaw and sent me tumbling backwards. Pinpoints of light flashed in my vision.

I shook my head and fired again. The ogre was getting annoyed as he leaped at me. I barely dodged the life-ending stomp but not the pile-driver fist. I managed two more shots as the ogre kicked me, smashing my side and launching me down the street. Only my duster saved me from being broken in several places.

"Your weapon is useless against me, wizard," the ogre said as he closed in on me again.

"I was just thinking the same thing," I said with a grunt. "It could be someone sold me bad ammo… or sometimes they just need a jumpstart." I gestured, traced a rune in the air, and nearly passed out from the pain. A black rune slammed into the ogre.

"You're a dark mage?" it said with a howl as it began clawing at the bullet wounds.

"As dark as they come," I said, wiping the blood from my lips. The entropy rounds exploded inside the ogre, disintegrating large sections of its body. Seconds later, nothing was left of the ogre except a pile of dust.

With the imminent threat gone, the woman snapped out of her shock. She shuffled to me slowly, clutching her bag in two hands, and keeping it to close to her body.

"Are you okay?" She inspected me from a safe distance, and I didn't blame her. "You don't look so good."

"Thanks." I leaned against the wall to stop the spinning. "What the hell are you doing out here in the first place?"

"Milk…I needed milk for my—"

"No." I held up a hand and winced as a lance of fresh agony shot up my side and stole my breath. "Don't want to know and don't care. Get off the street before more rummers show up and ghost you."

"Thank you," she mumbled. "You saved my life."

I looked at her then. "I'm not the hero you wanted —I'm the monster you needed," I said. "You want to thank me? Get your ass home and stay home."

"I still need the milk."

"Your funeral." I limped out of the dead-end and turned the corner as she ran in the other direction. I hung back a few seconds and shadowed her until she got home, and locked the door behind her. As I stumbled into The Dive, I made a mental note to have a conversation with Tessa about the delay on the entropy rounds as I stumbled into The Dive.

***

The Dive attracted a specific kind of clientele, mostly mages and other magic-users who didn't want to be bothered by the Dark Council. On occasion, we would get one of the other supernaturals. The building was located in what was once called Alphabet City, on 4th Street between Avenue C and D.

I was pretty sure I took two steps before my face met the floor. The manager, Cole, who looked more like a bouncer, rushed over.

"What mess did you stumble into this time, Grey?" Cole muttered under his breath as he slowly flipped me over onto my back with a grunt.

I owned The Dive. I used it as my informal base of operations. Mostly it served as a supernatural bar. Think Cheers but where *nobody* wants to know your name.

The Dive always tasted like bitter honey to me, the ambient magic a mix of minor traps and lethal failsafes.

It was the official unofficial neutral zone in this part of the city. I had a small apartment upstairs and enough runes to fry any magic-user thinking of casting inside its walls. It also had a state-of-the-art security system. There was only one rule in The Dive: Drink in peace or leave in pieces. Frank made sure the rule was enforced.

"I need a drink," I said through the pain that nearly blinded me. "Something strong like battery acid."

"Grey, you look like something I would vomit," Frank said from the bar. "Check that. You look like *old* vomit."

"Good to see you too, Frank," I said with a grunt. "I would step on you, but why ruin a good boot?"

The eight-inch thorny dragon hissed at me from the top of the bar. Frank was—according to the rumors— the result of a transmutation spell gone wrong. No one knew for sure, and Frank had a different story every time someone asked. At this point, I don't think even he remembered. Being trapped in the body of a thorny dragon would make me irritable and cranky all the time too.

"Stryder, you need a hospital," Cole said, pulling out a phone. "I'm calling Roxanne."

"She's going to be pissed." I closed my eyes. "Do me a favor and just shoot me now."

"Hope she fries your ass for casting," Frank said with a laugh and stalked off. "You do realize your expiration date is coming up? I can read the stone now: Grey Stryder-death at the hands of one pissed off sorcereress. He never saw it coming."

I gave Frank my one-fingered answer.

"You cast?" Cole hissed, "She's going to be more

than pissed—and it's your own damn fault."

That's when I passed out.

TWO

THE BRIGHT HOSPITAL lights burned into my eyes. An angry Roxanne De Marco came into my field of vision a second later.

"Hey, Rox." I tried to sit up, but my brain belayed the order and my body remained prone. "You're looking good."

"Shut it." She held a clipboard and narrowed her eyes at me. "You used magic? What part of 'you are dying' is unclear to you?"

"There was a woman, she was in trouble—"

"There will always be someone in trouble, Grey!" she yelled and slammed the clipboard on the side table. "You can't save everyone."

"I wasn't going to let her die, either," I said. "Not on my watch."

"The Night Wardens are obsolete." She crossed her arms, staring at me. "The NYTF and Dark Council—"

"Weren't there last night to save her—I was." I pulled my hand away. "How are you and Mr. Tea and Crumpets?"

"We're good, Grey." She glared at me with a shake of her head. "His name is Tristan, and I told you, he's a perfect gentleman."

"He'd better be or else I'm—"

"Stop trying to change the subject," she said, standing. "I'm not some defenseless waif. Besides, my personal relations are exactly that—personal. You would do well to remember that."

"Yes, ma'am," I said with a smile. "How long until I can get out of here? You know I hate hospitals. They taste like old coffee."

"I'm thinking of keeping you here a few days," she said with mock seriousness. "Or until you come to your senses, whichever happens first."

"C'mon, Rox," I said. "A few days? I can't do a few days in here."

"If you cast again, with your condition…," she started.

"I promise, no more magic." I held my hands up in surrender. "From now on, it's only Fatebringer and stern words."

She rolled her eyes at me. "Until you see someone else in trouble, and then you'll cast," she said, pointing a finger at me. "I swear I should tell Tristan."

"That wouldn't end well," I said. "He would try and detain, or worse, help me. We both know how well that worked last time."

"Grey, casting will kill you—no more magic."

"Fine, no more magic," I said, giving in. "When can I leave?"

"I'm keeping you here for observation." She looked at the clipboard again. "Be thankful it's only two nights."

She approached me with a cup and a tablet. "Drink this, it will help you sleep. At the very least it should dull the magisthesia."

"Sleep?" I said, stretching out my arms with a wince. "I feel great."

"Would you like to feel horrible?" she asked, her voice steel. "Take this and drink."

I took the tablet and drank the contents of the cup. Rox was no slouch, and I didn't have the energy to argue with her about this—especially when she was right.

She left the room with a smile and a wave. I cursed silently. The only thing that preventing me from escaping, aside from the multitude of runes, was my respect for our deep friendship. She was one of the few people I trusted with my life. I would give her one night and then I was gone.

THREE

I AWOKE AND moved before I remembered the state my body was in. Pain flared everywhere, and I laid my head back with a groan. Someone was in my room. The lights were dimmed and I could just make out a figure sitting in the corner.

"Grey Stryder," said a voice. "Do you know why I'm paying you a visit?"

I recognized the voice. I focused my vision and saw the other figure I knew would be there. Hades rarely traveled alone. My senses were quiet, which meant either he was completely masked, or the meds Rox had given me were kicking into overdrive.

"You're bored?" I finally said.

"I don't get bored. I'm here because I need action taken. This new strain of Redrum has caused a significant disruption to my operations."

"You don't need me, you have the manpower for that." I peered into the darkness at his head of security, Corbel. I'd heard the stories about the supposed 'Hound of Hades.' I wasn't impressed.

"I need someone unaffiliated and unfettered." Hades steepled his fingers. "Not bound to the Council, the NYTF, or anyone else for that matter. Not even to me."

"I think the word you're looking for is expendable," I said with a short laugh, and regretted it as the pain squeezed a gasp out of me. "You do realize I'm a Night Warden?"

"Not according to the Night Wardens."

"It's a simple miscommunication." I shifted in the bed to alleviate some of the pain. "They frown upon the use of dark magic."

"That dark magic is the reason you're dying."

"Tell me something I don't know."

"You've chosen to live unattached," Hades said, as if saying it softly made the pain of loss easier. "No family, no friends, no loved ones—you're alone."

"I have friends."

"No one of consequence."

"You're wasting my time." I sat up with a grimace and looked at him. He was in his typical banker suit, looking like he bathed in money. "Time I don't have, as you so subtly stated."

"What if I could help you?"

I stared at him. I'd heard this pitch before. 'I'll cure you if you come work for me'—except it was always bullshit.

"No one can help me," I said. "What I have has no cure, but you know that."

"Indeed, so what do you have to lose?"

"I think the better question is what do you have to gain?" I adjusted to get a better look at him. "Why help me?"

"It serves my purposes."

Gods and their games. Supernaturals always thought they were superior to normals—including the heavy-hitters like Hades. Especially them.

He reached down and handed Corbel what looked like a long stick. Corbel stepped closer and placed the object at the foot of the bed. It was a sword in a scabbard.

"Going away present?" Its essence was a mixture of dark chocolate mixed with black coffee. Serious magic laced with lethal runes. The kind of thing I made a point of staying away from.

"If you like," Hades said as Corbel stepped back. "That sword will stop the ravages of your illness."

"My illness, as you call it, is the consequence of a massive entropy spell gone wrong. A sword can't help with that, nothing can—unless you want me to fall on it." I looked at the scabbard. Part of me wanted him to be telling the truth, but I knew better. "Nothing can."

"This is no ordinary sword, Mr. Stryder." Hades leaned back and looked off to the side. "Just like you are no ordinary Warden."

"I'm blushing here—why me?"

"A dark blade for a dark mage," Hades said with a wave of his hand. "It has a certain symmetry."

"Dark blade?" I shook my head. "Hell no—no offense. A dark blade is just another word for *fucked*. I'm dying, but I'm not looking to rush the journey. I take that blade and it accelerates the process by painting a large target on my forehead and back. I'll pass, but thanks."

"If you don't take it, I'm sure I can find another suitable candidate—perhaps another of the Night Wardens?" Hades said with a smile as he leaned forward. "Maybe one of the ones who don't want to kill you. Oh, wait, they all want you dead, don't they?"

"Have I ever told you what a right bastard you are?" Corbel tensed up, and Hades raised a hand, stopping his Hound.

"You remind me of someone we both know, who also has the tendency to let his words take him into potentially lethal situations." Hades motioned for Corbel to return to the wall.

"Who's a good Hound?" I said, and Corbel stiffened as he returned to where he'd been stationed. "What's the catch? There's always a cost."

"Always," Hades said while leaning back. "Remove the Redrum users from the streets, and find the suppliers of this new strain. After that, the sword is yours to keep and do with as you see fit."

"Too easy," I said. "I don't need a sword for that."

"True." Hades nodded and pointed. "Soon you will have Charon escorting you off this plane. If you are bound to this sword, you can prevent that."

"Bound?" I scoffed. "I don't do commitment well. That sounds long-term."

"The sword requires a host, a life force to draw from," he said. "I'm told the benefits far outweigh the costs. In your case, one benefit would be prolonged life. Especially since I hear casting can be fatal these days."

I looked at the scabbard. I wasn't in a hurry to die, but I had made peace with the idea. How long did I have? One or maybe two years if I didn't use magic. No one knew for sure. But taking it meant being connected to a weapon for the rest of my life.

"And if I don't want it?"

"Feel free to return it."

"I don't take orders from anyone," I said, shifting in the bed. "I don't work for you, the NYTF or the Dark Council. I do this my way. I work alone."

"I only ask that you cleanse the streets of our city from this vile poison." Hades stood and then took a step closer. "I do have one caveat."

Here it was—the catch.

"I have an agent who has become unsuitable for her line of work. I need you to adjust her sensibilities."

"I work alone." I leaned back and crossed my arms. "If she works for you, she needs more than an adjustment—she needs an intervention."

"How was this evening's patrol?" He extended a hand, examining his fingernails. "You did manage to save the woman and destroy the 'rummer,' as you call them? Did you notice anything odd about the creature?"

"I did fine." My voice caught as the pain crept up my side. "Handled it pretty well."

"And yet it required three LIT rounds to dispatch. Is this common?"

"I must have gotten defective rounds from Tessa," I lied. Tessa only sold the highest quality illegal goods. One round should have put the rummer down—not three.

"Of course, that must be it." I saw his eyes glow a subtle violet in the dim room. "It's a good thing the ogre only managed to inflict minor injuries. If only you had someone to assist you in your rescues."

"I...work...alone," I said through gasps as the pain increased. "This isn't exactly motivating me to agree."

"Very well," Hades said with a sigh. He signaled to Corbel, who approached the sword. "Enjoy your remaining years. I apologize for wasting your incredibly limited time. I'll make sure she is given a proper retirement."

Goddammit. I've seen what passes for retirement with Hades. It's painful right up until the point it becomes fatal. He would ghost her without a second thought. Corbel narrowed his eyes at me. I knew that look, and damn straight, he would owe me.

"She does what I say when I say," I said with a sigh, knowing I was going to regret this. "She sasses me, or gives me attitude, she's gone."

Corbel stopped next to the bed and gave me a short nod.

"I would expect no less from a Night Warden of your stature," Hades said with a smile as he brushed off his suit.

"Stop blowing smoke up my ass—the Wardens can't wait until I'm a memory," I said, looking at him. "What's the name?"

"Her name is Koda," he said. "I suggest a firm hand. Her previous handler"—he glanced at Corbel, who scowled—"allowed her an exorbitant amount of latitude."

"I'll keep that in mind. Is she street-skilled, or do I have to teach her how to stay alive?"

"She worked for me, Mr. Stryder. She is

exceptionally skilled in staying alive."

"So skilled you're pushing her on me like rotten meat," I answered. "If she gets ghosted out there, it's on her."

Hades sighed. "She lacks discipline and a certain ruthlessness. Something I'm certain you can provide her instruction in."

He knew. The bastard knew I was going to take his deal. I leaned forward, my body protesting in pain, and grabbed the scabbard. The sword jumped in my hand.

"What the—?"

"The blade's full name is *Kuro kokoro kokutan no ken* which is loosely translated into 'dark spirit'." He gestured, and Corbel reached into a pocket, produced a small book, and placed it near me on the bed. "This is as much of the history of the blade as I could obtain. After all, knowledge is power. Study it."

"What do I have to lose?" I picked up the book and noticed the runic failsafes inscribed on the cover.

"Indeed. Koda will arrive tomorrow," Hades said. "I would consider investigating why it took three LIT rounds to dispatch the rummer."

"I'll look into it." It had been on my mind. If they were becoming UV-resistant, we were in for a world of pain. "I need to go see Tessa."

"An excellent idea." With a gesture, Hades and Corbel disappeared.

FOUR

"YOU LOOK LIKE shit." The voice woke me, and I reached for Fatebringer. My body reminded me about playing with angry ogres by sending a wave of cascading pain up and down my side. "Good reflexes though."

She was thin and wiry. Her long, cascading black hair had red streaks in it. I could tell that it hadn't seen a brush or comb in a long time. Her pale skin seemed almost translucent, and she sat well back from the sunlight that bathed the room. A thin visor hid her eyes. I noticed she was dressed in assassin leathers and boots.

I cursed Rox for leaving the blinds open. On the side table, next to my guest, I saw Fatebringer disassembled and broken down into several small parts. The protective runes should've prevented her from tampering with it, much less taking it apart. I didn't get anything else from her, which threw me. Everyone has an energy signature, but hers was missing.

"It's rude to grab a man's weapon without

permission." I sat up in the bed slowly. "How did you get around the runes?"

"What happened to you?" she said, looking down at the pieces and scrunching her face. "I thought you were some badass. Looks like you got your ass kicked or a truck hit you—a few times. Maybe both."

I thought back to the ogre who'd wanted to rearrange my everything and nodded. "Something like that." I pointed at the pieces of Fatebringer. "You're going to have to put that back toget—"

Her hands blurred over the pieces as she reassembled Fatebringer. I mentally timed her at ten seconds. Which had to be wrong, since no one was that fast. Especially with a runed weapon. She slid it back to me butt first with a nod.

"Nice gun, but it's a little on the light side." She looked at the scabbard. "Where did you get entropy rounds? I thought those were banned?"

"What the hell are you?" I managed after a few seconds of shock. "You aren't supposed to be able to do that. No one is."

She lowered the visor. Her eyes gave off a faint red glow, as she smiled at me. "Not even Night Wardens?"

"You touch my gun again, I'll shoot you myself." I grabbed Fatebringer, checked it, and made sure it was functional. "Don't touch any of my weapons—ever."

I was about to say more, when a cough from the door interrupted me. Roxanne entered the room and glanced at the assassin before grabbing my chart.

"I see you have a guest." Roxanne looked over my chart and gave me a routine examination. "Does your guest have a name?"

"Sure, it's 'pain in my—'" I started.

"Koda, ma'am," she said, standing up and extending a hand. "You must be Haven Director DeMarco. Pleased to meet you. I'm here to assist Night Warden Stryder."

Roxanne raised an eyebrow as she took Koda's hand and shook it.

"I thought you worked alone?" Roxanne said, turning to me with a smile. "She has manners and looks capable. Clearly there must be some mistake if she's going to work with you."

"I do," I said with a growl. "She's on extended probation. I'm not sure she's going to make it."

"Do keep her." Roxanne placed the chart on the side table. "If only to limit your visits here."

"You say that like I'm here every night," I said with a scowl. "I do manage to patrol without getting hurt."

"Until someone is in danger, and then you lose all sense of self-preservation." Roxanne looked Koda over. "Are you a Night Warden, Koda?"

"Not yet, ma'am," Koda said, looking at me.

"I told you she's on probation. Besides, you know the Night Wardens aren't adding to their ranks anymore, remember? We're obsolete."

"I've been trying to get him to leave the Wardens for years." Roxanne opened a closet and pulled out a bundle. "Maybe you can succeed where I've failed."

I groaned in response. I knew where this was headed.

"Rox…" I said, trying to head off the impending rant.

She held up a hand and ignored me.

"Maybe you'll have more luck," she said. "Whatever you do, don't become a Warden. All they do is roam around the streets at night, looking for trouble." She stared at me hard. "And they usually find it."

"I'll do my best to avoid trouble, ma'am." Koda sat down and looked at me.

"You won't avoid it for long if you're on the streets with him," Roxanne said, pointing at me. "I hope you're skilled, at least."

Roxanne dropped the bundle of clothes and my duster on the bed, and picked up the scabbard. I felt the energy of the sword, and Roxanne narrowed her eyes at me.

"Since when do you use a sword?"

"I don't," I said quickly. "I'm just—"

She took the hilt and drew the blade. The runes on the black blade gleamed in the sunlight. Red runes flashed. I felt the energy in the room shift and I grabbed the scabbard, pushing the blade back in. The smell of coffee filled the room.

"Not a good idea, Rox."

"Where did you get that blade, Grey?" Roxanne had formed an orb of red energy in her opposite hand. "Don't you dare lie to me."

The bass tone that rumbled in my stomach made me queasy. I knew she was serious. The meds were screwing with my senses. Magic usually only affected tones and taste. The blade, Roxanne using magic, and the meds were causing sensory crossovers.

"Hades," I said under my breath. "I'm just holding it for him."

"Are you insane?" She absorbed the orb and stepped

closer to the bed, grabbing my shirt. "That blade is dangerous. Give it back—now."

"Not yet." I put the scabbard next to me on the bed. "I have to see if he was telling the truth."

"The truth?" she said, crossing her arms. "The truth about what?"

"He said it can stop the entropic dissolution."

"And you believe him." Her face was a stone mask. "He's a god, Grey. Everything is half-truths with them. You cast that spell and lost everything. Don't trust him."

"I know. I'll do it on my terms, Rox."

"And her?" Roxanne glanced over at Koda. "Is she part of this too?"

"Unrelated," I said, my voice steel. "Just need someone to watch my six. Like you said—I'm good at finding trouble."

I could tell Roxanne remained unconvinced, but she nodded. "Simon has a blade that looks like that. Maybe you should speak to—"

"No, thanks." I held up a hand and shook my head. "He's actually okay, at least compared to Tea and Crumpets, but I'll pass. Besides, I need to go see Tessa."

"The Moving Market?" Roxanne narrowed her eyes. "Who said you were cleared to leave Haven?"

"I did." I grabbed my clothes and stood. "Can I have a little privacy, ladies?"

"Who do you think treats you when you end up in here like mangled hamburger?"

"That nurse on the third floor who keeps giving me the looks?" I said, wagging my eyebrows. "You know the one?"

"Dream on." Roxanne waved her hand at me and grabbed my chart. "Let's go, Koda. Mr. Stryder would like some privacy."

They left the room and I got dressed. I put the runed book about the sword in one of my coat's secret pockets. I grabbed the sword, and it jumped again.

"Shit." I placed it in another pocket of my special duster. "Nothing good will come of this."

FIVE

"WHY DIDN'T YOU tell her about me?" Koda asked when we arrived at the garage level. "You didn't tell her about my working for Hades."

"Rox is the closest I'll get to family." I pressed the special fob, and my bike shimmered into view. "If I told her about you, she'd be upset. That woman is dangerous when she's upset."

"So you lied?" Koda asked as she approached my bike. "Is this an Ecosse?"

"I didn't lie," I said with a scowl. "I opted not to get into a knockdown, drag-out battle with one of the most powerful sorceresses I know. It was preservation —yours and mine. You're welcome, by the way."

"So you're scared of her?"

"If you were smart, you would be, too." I placed my hand on the side of the Shroud. It was a SuNaTran— Supernatural Transport—variant of the Ecosse superbike, outfitted with extras, like camouflage and biometric locks. The side panel flared with orange runes and the engine started as I jumped on. Koda looked around. "I only have one. Get on or walk."

"No helmets?" Koda asked, getting on the back.

"Always." I put on my glasses and handed her a pair. They flared violet for a second and a kinetic buffer surrounded my head. "This is a kinetic buffer. Think helmet, but without the helmet. Put them on. They're audio linked."

"Impressive," she said, swapping glasses and wrapping her arms around my waist as we pulled off. "Where are we going? Who's Tessa?"

"She runs the Market now after Nick got himself retired a while back."

"The Market?"

I pulled a hard right and jumped on the FDR, swerving around traffic as I headed uptown. According to my calculations, I needed to get to 86th Street within the next thirty minutes, or I'd have to head downtown for the Hudson Yards entrance.

"The Moving Market is where I get my ammo, among other things," I said. "I need to ask Tessa why it took three LIT rounds to put down a rummer, when it should only take one."

"Are you sure you hit it the first two times?" she asked, and I could almost hear the smile. "Could be you're a lousy shot or the ammo is shit. I hear LIT rounds are unstable."

"I don't miss, and Tessa sells only the highest quality ammo."

"You don't miss—which I doubt, but let's say it's true—and only get the best ammo," she said. "That only leaves one other option."

"What? Rummers are becoming resistant to LIT

rounds?"

"Once you eliminate the impossible, whatever remains, however improbable, must be the truth," she said, as I slipped between two cars and took the 86th Street exit. "But I seriously doubt you don't miss. It was dark. You were facing a rummer, it would be easy to miss twice."

"Not at point-blank range."

I felt her shrug her shoulders. "Even I could miss at point-blank with an angry ogre coming at me," she said as we pulled up to Carl Schurz Park. I parked the Shroud and activated its camouflage. It shimmered and disappeared from view.

"Let's go." I entered the park and headed up the stairs to the promenade that looked over the East River. Next to the benches sat a small maintenance building. I looked around the promenade for a few seconds. Memories of sitting on the bench with Jade and watching the boats travel up and down the river rushed back—a cruel reminder of the price she paid, and how alone I was.

"Hello?" Koda waved her hand in front of my eyes. "Anyone home?"

"What?" I growled, irritated that I had let my guard down enough for the past to blindside me.

"I was saying, what if someone bumps into the bike?" Koda asked as I stepped over to the door of the small building.

"It's not just camouflage." I looked down at my watch. In a few minutes, the Market entrance would arrive. "The Shroud actually phases out of this plane and remains in-between planes."

"Like a plane weaver." She looked back to where I parked the bike. "But if you can't cast—"

"Who said I *can't*?" I placed my hand on the door handle. "I *choose* not to."

"Right." She looked around the empty promenade. "It has nothing to do with you accelerating an entropic dissolution every time you use magic. That must be a coincidence. How did you manage to cast that spell? It requires at least two mages."

I glared at her. "Anyone ever tell you that you talk too much?"

"Only those trying to avoid the subject."

"I was the lucky one." My thoughts raced back to Jade. "In the end I had to finish it—alone."

"Stryder, don't lie to me," she said, and stared back. "I either work with you or I face retirement. This is no picnic for me. If you drop dead because you're too stupid to live—I go back to Hades. This isn't just about you."

"Which could still happen," I said, angry at being confronted. "This"—I waved my hand between us —"isn't permanent, you know."

"Listen, let's not waste each other's time." She crossed her arms and blocked the door. "If you want me gone, just say the word and I'm a memory. I can always go underground and off-grid."

"Off-grid. From Hades?" I shook my head. "You do realize Hades is a god? One of the old ones?"

"I can do it." Her confidence sounded shaky at best. "No one will find me."

"Because your body will be scattered in the wind," I muttered. "There won't be much left to find."

"I have a way." She stared at me with her arms crossed. "There's a way to do it."

"You don't know what you're talking about." I stared at her hard. "There is nowhere you can hide from Hades or Corbel. They call him the 'Hound of Hades' for a reason and it's not because he's cute and cuddly."

"I'm resourceful," she said. "There are places they won't find me."

"Sooner or later he will." I shook my head at her naiveté. "And once he does, he'll ghost you in a heartbeat."

I remembered the last agent Hades retired. I pushed the image from my mind. No one deserved that kind of *retirement*.

"At least with him I know where I stand, instead of your passive-aggressive bullshit," she said, pointing at my chest. "You agreed to help me or I wouldn't be here. Own it and let's move on."

I looked at her in mild shock. I could see why Hades wanted to unload her. She was a monumental hemorrhoid.

"Did you speak to Hades or Corbel like this?"

"Like what?" she said, looking at me innocently. "This is how I speak."

"You either have a deathwish or are good at what you do."

"I'm not good—I'm the best," she said, looking away. "At least I was."

"Nevermind. You're here, we'll make it work. Now shut up, let me concentrate, and get out of my way."

I took off my glasses and focused on the door. I couldn't cast without agonizing pain, but I could direct small amounts of magic to activate the Market locks. I placed my hand on the door and let a trickle of energy flow. An aftertaste of lime flooded my tongue.

"Fine," she said, holding her hands up in mock surrender. She stepped to the side and looked at the small building. "This place looks a little small for any kind of market."

"It's bigger on the inside." I felt the shift in energy as the entrance arrived. "Especially now."

A bright light flashed at the edges of the door for half a second. I turned the handle and motioned for her to enter. I followed into a large foyer. Even though I no longer wielded magic actively, the door could read my runic signature. If anyone besides a magic-user opened the door, the inside of the maintenance shack was all they would see.

We stood in Market Central. The entire market was arranged as a wheel formed of seven concentric circles.

"I've heard of these places," Koda said, looking around. "This is a time and relative dimension in space pocket, right?"

"Something like that, only a little more complicated," I said as we entered the building in front of us. "Tessa keeps it shifting in the interstices of a few seconds. Don't ask me how. All I know is that she'll have the answers about the defective rounds."

This building, which also doubled as Tessa's main office, acted as the hub of the wheel. The seven rings were arranged in order of influence and power.

The higher ranked magic-users inhabited the rings closest to the hub. The two outer rings were a no-man's land. Exploring the outer rings meant one of two things: you were there to be killed or to do some killing. There was one law in the Market. Only the strong, clever, and ruthless survived. I was all three.

A short woman approached us. She was dressed in a casual business suit, and she held a clipboard. Her nametag read Eileen.

"Welcome, Mr. Stryder. How can we serve you today?"

"I need to speak to Tessa."

The woman checked her clipboard and shook her head slowly. "I'm sorry. Ms. Wract is busy in meetings until the end of the day," Eileen said apologetically. "Perhaps I could schedule for another day? Do you need to purchase some ammunition?"

I kept my frustration in check and smiled. It wasn't my fault my facial muscles weren't used to the expression. Eileen took a step back, and I stopped trying to be friendly.

"A rummer nearly disemboweled me because I had to use *three* LIT rounds to put it down—rounds that I bought here."

"Three?" Eileen asked with a look of surprise. "Are you certain you didn't just miss the first two times?"

Koda snorted next to me, giving me a smug look and an 'I told you so' shrug.

"I don't miss," I said, irritated. I glanced at Koda. "Unless it's on purpose."

"I meant no disrespect, Mr. Stryder," Eileen answered quickly. "It's just that we sell top of the line munitions. Three rounds to stop a Redrum user... seems excessive."

"Imagine the reaction when I start telling the other

Wardens that the Market is selling defective ammunition," I lied. The other Wardens would probably shoot first and not bother with questions if I ever approached them, but Eileen didn't know that. "I would expect sales to drop a bit, wouldn't you?"

"I'll contact Ms. Wract," Eileen said, pulling out a phone. "Please give me a moment. Would you be so kind as to wait in the reception area?"

"Good idea." I looked in the direction she pointed.

Eileen directed us to an open area with tables and large sofas. A few desks were situated against the walls. Behind one large desk stood another woman dressed in an identical suit Eileen wore.

"Can't you get these rounds somewhere else?" Koda asked as we moved over to the main reception space. I settled into one of the large leather sofas. "What's the big deal?"

"It takes me an extra three seconds to fire three rounds instead of one." I scanned the reception area. "Three seconds can be the difference between walking away and bleeding out in a dirty alley. Not dying is a big deal to me."

"Not if you hit it the first time," she said with a smile. "You know—don't miss?"

"Don't say a word when Tessa arrives, understand?"

"Why not?"

"Get this now," I said with an edge, "Tessa doesn't have friends. She only cares about two things—Tessa and the Moving Market. The sooner you learn that, the longer you'll last in here. Are we clear?"

"Crystal," Koda said, sitting in one of the chairs. "I won't ask if they sell laser sights here—you know, to help with accuracy. Not that *you* need it, of course."

I grabbed a paperclip from one of the desks in the reception area. The space was done in minimalist art deco, with plenty of wood and stone surrounding the open area in the center. The subtle smell of lavender made me notice the vases filled with flowers on several of the wall stands.

I straightened out the clip and flung it at her. To her credit, she dodged it effortlessly. "I thought you didn't miss?" she said with a raised eyebrow. "Maybe they carry those prescription reading glasses here?"

"I didn't miss." I heard the door whisper open, but I didn't turn. "Remember what I said."

"Hello, Grey," said a voice from behind us. "It's good to see you again."

I stood and turned to face Tessa Wract—the new overseer of the Moving Market. She wore an expensive black Chanel pantsuit, which contrasted starkly against her white hair, giving her a dignified presence. Looking at her always reminded me of Helen Mirren, except with an extra dose of menace. She was slightly taller than Koda, but still stood under my chin. She gave me a pleasant smile, glanced over at Koda to assess any potential threat, and quickly dismissed her.

Her piercing hazel eyes shimmered with violet power as I took her hand and hoped Koda knew the meaning of restraint. Tessa was a time-weaver. It meant she could keep the Moving Market…moving. Not only did she slip it in-between planes, she was also powerful enough to move it through time. If she didn't want you to find the market, you didn't.

Before running the Market, she'd had some

unpleasant run-ins with mages working for the Dark Council. The last incident placed her in the current position of Market Overseer.

The rumors were that she had temporally stranded a mage in a conscious time loop who'd dared insult her. It forced the mage to repeat the same thirty seconds of his castration. She kept him there until he went mad, then she killed him.

It's obvious why I didn't want to piss her off.

"Tessa, the pleasure is always mine," I said.

She stepped back and looked me over. "You're looking well, Grey. I do wish you would let me get you a proper coat. This coat"—she gestured up and down at my duster—"makes you look like some wizard-for-hire from the Midwest."

"This was a gift from Aria." I pulled on my coat protectively. "She would be insulted if I replaced it."

Not to mention that I would be defenseless in what I considered hostile territory. She had been after my coat since Aria created it for me.

"I see it doubles as a runed holocaust cloak." Tessa narrowed her eyes at me. "Do you run into many dragons on your nightly patrols?"

"No, and I'd like to keep it that way."

"Very well," she said after a moment. "Let's discuss your matter in my office. Please bring your guest."

We followed her across the reception area. She stopped to remove the paper clip I thrown earlier.

"Grey," she said with a sigh, "I hire people for this sort of thing." She placed the clip in my hand. I held it up and handed it to Koda. Skewered on the end of it was a large fly. "Could you please refrain from target practice?"

The look on Koda's face was worth Tessa's chastising. We left the reception area as Tessa placed a hand on the wall. A section slid back and we entered her office.

Tessa's office was a large, expansive area. Neat stacks of paper covered her behemoth Parnian desk. Set in front of it were two large leather chairs. The walls were bare, except for a large reproduction of Dali's *The Persistence of Memory*. A smaller version of the same work sat on her desk.

"Nice reproduction," I said, admiring the piece on her desk.

"That's the original. The reproduction is on the wall." Tessa sat behind her desk. "I went back and had Salva paint me that one."

"I thought the original was in MoMA?" I sat in one of the large chairs facing her. Koda sat in the other. Upon closer inspection, I realized I was sitting in a Dragons armchair. "Is this a—?"

"Did you come here to catalogue my office furniture?" Tessa said with a tight smile. "Or threaten the Market with exposure for subpar merchandise?"

"Eileen wasn't cooperating, and I needed to speak with you."

"Don't threaten my staff or the Market—ever," she said, and sitting back in her chair. "You have no idea what I've had to do after Nick got himself removed for dealing with Blood Hunters. The last thing I need are baseless threats. Clear?"

"Completely," I said with an edge in my voice. Tessa was no slouch, and in a fair fight, she would be difficult to confront. We had an ongoing *détente* because she knew I never fought fair. "Maybe you can explain why it took three rounds instead of one to put down a rummer?"

"May I see your weapon?" She held out her hand and turned to Koda. "And who is this young woman?"

I unholstered Fatebringer and placed it on her desk. Tessa rarely asked a question she didn't know the answer to. This was a test.

"Her name is Koda." She ejected the round in the chamber and slid Fatebringer back to me. I left it on the desk. "Used to work for Hades as a cleaner, I'm guessing."

"I'm thinking she did more than just *cleaning*," Tessa speculated. "Koda?" Tessa examined one of the rounds closely. "As in granddaughter of Kano the Fan, of the infamous Hand of Fate?"

I saw Koda stiffen, clench her jaw, and nod. Tessa glanced up at her reaction and smiled.

"Surprised?" Tessa asked, standing the round on the desk and waving her hand over it. It separated into several components. "Don't be. Kano was a fierce friend and fiercer fighter. Though I don't think he would've been pleased to find you working for Hades."

"She doesn't," I said quickly. "At least not anymore."

Tessa raised an eyebrow at my words and nodded when I didn't elaborate. "A granddaughter of Kano can only mean you wield the *tessen*," Tessa said, leaving me confused. "Do you have them?"

Koda hesitated and glanced at me. I nodded. She gestured and produced two slim, rectangular pieces of metal, about a foot long each. She placed them on top of the desk and slid them forward. They looked harmless.

"You're thinking these are just harmless pieces of metal," Tessa said, looking at me and resting a finger on one of the metal rectangles. "In the right hands, these are devastating weapons. May I?"

Koda gave her a slight nod.

"Not really seeing it." I shook my head as Tessa held one of the rectangles and flicked her wrist. It opened with a metallic ring into a black fan covered in red runes. The edge of the fan appeared to be razor sharp. I saw that each metal rib contained a slim, retractable dagger.

"Seeing it now?" Tessa asked. "Iron fans are the ultimate weapon of defense and offense combined."

The runes on the surface of the fan trailed red energy as Tessa moved it slowly through the air. I couldn't make them all out, but what I did read filled me with a healthy respect. There were extensive protective runes, along with some nasty runes of sharpness. The muscles in Koda's jaw flexed as her eyes tracked the motion of the fan.

"Definitely seeing it now," I muttered, wary of where Tessa waved the fan. "How about we return them to their owner?"

"These are Kano's *tessen*." Tessa admired the fan, turning it. "To wield these means you possess skill. Why are you with Grey?"

"You make that sound like it's a bad thing."

"It's not a step up." Tessa slid the fan back to Koda. "Why did Hades dismiss you?"

Koda looked away as she took her fans and made

them disappear into her sleeves with a flick of her wrist. "I failed an assignment, and Corbel had to step in," Koda looked away into a memory. "It was—"

Tessa held up a hand. "Nevermind," she said. "Consider yourself fortunate you weren't *retired.* Although working with Grey isn't much better."

"No one knows my heritage," Koda said. "Not even Hades knows all of it."

"I'm not Hades." Tessa turned back and looked at me. "The LIT round is fully functional as far as I can tell. I know your aim is impeccable as ever, which leaves only one explanation."

"Rummers are becoming UV-resistant?" I said in disbelief. "Well, that's all kinds of bad."

SIX

"IF THEY ARE becoming resistant to LIT rounds, it's only a matter of time before they grow out of control," Tessa said. "How many hard-to-kill rummers have you encountered?"

"Just one so far." I took Fatebringer from the desk and holstered it. "It was running with an ogre. Never seen that before either. Usually they're in packs."

Tessa leaned back, tapping her lip with her forefinger as she looked at the Dali on the wall.

"A UV-resistant vampire would threaten the entire city," Tessa said. "This sounds like someone making a power play."

"Hades mentioned something about Redrum." I glanced at Koda, who was recovering from Tessa's questioning. "Do you know anything about this new strain?"

Tessa's face hardened as she stared at me.

"We deal in many things here in the Market—some of questionable legality," she said, never taking her eyes off me. "Redrum is not one of them."

"Not even the outer rings?" I asked. "You know the Market is a big place. Those outer rings can be a bit hard to control. Nick could never—"

"I like you, Grey, which is why I'm going to ignore that question and the implicit accusation," Tessa said quietly, the temperature of the room dropping by a few degrees. "When I say Redrum isn't trafficked in the Market—I mean the *entire* market."

I knew better than to push her. I stood and gave her a slight bow. She remained behind her desk. Violet energy raced across her irises as her eyes followed me.

"Thank you for your time, Tessa," I said, adjusting my duster. "Maybe I need to ask someone else."

"I heard keepsakers were recently used to hold Redrum." Tessa stood and placed a hand on her desk. A section glowed violet. Across the office, the exit opened. "Perhaps the Smiths know more. Give my regards to Aria."

"I'll do that." I stepped to one side as she escorted us halfway and stood in the center of her office. "Thanks again, Tess."

"Grey, if you call me that again, I'll leave your wretched ass trapped in a time loop," she said with a smile that never reached her eyes. "It won't be pleasant —for you."

I shivered in response and shook my head.

"No, thanks. I've heard of your time loops."

"Eileen will have some more ammunition for you on your way out," she said and turned back to her desk with a wave. "I have a feeling you're going to need it. Come visit me when you're ready to upgrade that atrocity you call a coat. Oh—and Koda?"

We stopped walking. "Yes?" Koda said as she tensed.

"Your grandfather died a warrior's death, even though few remember it," Tessa said, leaning against the edge of her desk and staring at Koda. "Make sure you honor his memory."

"I will." Koda gave her a slight bow and stepped out of the office.

I stepped into the reception area and the wall whispered closed behind me. Eileen approached and handed me a large case.

"Ms. Wract said you would be needing these." She placed the case on one of the desks.

"How much?" I snapped it open and saw various types of ammo. There was enough to last me a year. "Does Tessa think I'm going to war?"

Koda looked over my shoulder and whistled. "That's a lot of ammunition for someone who doesn't miss," she said with a smile as I glared at her.

"Ms. Wract believes in preparation and planning," Eileen answered. "If you fail to plan, you plan to fail."

"I don't see entropy rounds." I closed the case and looked at Eileen. "Out of stock?"

Eileen shook her head. "As we both know, entropy rounds are considered contraband." She pointed at a group of boxes in the case. "Negation rounds. More powerful than entropy rounds and tailored to your pistol."

"More powerful, but not illegal?" I asked, grabbing a handful and filling three of the speed loaders next to the box of ammunition and dropping them into a pocket. "How does she manage that?"

"Not illegal or recognized at the moment by the

NYTF or Dark Council," Eileen replied. "Therefore not contraband."

"Of course not," I said, realizing that the loophole was typical for the Moving Market. "At least not yet."

"The ammunition is courtesy of Ms. Wract and the Market." Eileen looked down at a clipboard. "I trust you know the way out?"

I nodded. "Tell Tessa I said thank you." I grabbed the case and placed it inside one of the duster's pockets.

Koda raised an eyebrow at my duster.

Eileen nodded curtly. "Have a good day, Mr. Stryder," she said and walked off.

"Their customer service could use some work," Koda said, grabbing the edge of my duster. "Where did you put it?"

"Put what?"

"That was a lot of ammo," she muttered to herself. "Yet no weight transference to the coat. Impressive."

She examined both sides of the duster, moving it back and forth. I pulled the coat from her grip and headed back to the main entrance with Koda keeping pace. I grabbed the handle and the edge of the doorframe flashed white for a split second.

We stepped through the threshold and back into the maintenance shack at Carl Schurz Park.

SEVEN

"WELL, THAT WAS a waste of time," Koda said, clearly frustrated. "How did she know about me and my past?"

"What did you learn from the visit?" I looked over to the Roosevelt Island Lighthouse as we stepped onto the promenade. "Or were you just focused on what she told you about your grandfather?"

I stood still and let my senses expand. It was an old Night Warden skill I used to make sure an area was clear of threats. The promenade was empty except for us.

I looked out over the water one last time and headed down the stairs. Koda trailed behind me in silence. I knew she was still off-balance about Tessa, but she would need to learn to recover fast if she was going to survive on the streets of this city.

"So you didn't learn anything?" I asked.

"Of course I did," she snapped back. "She doesn't like you much."

"Who, Tessa or Eileen?"

"Tessa. I just don't know why she deals with you if she doesn't."

"We have—*history*." I pressed the fob in my pocket and the Shroud shimmered into view. "I'm a living reminder of a past she's trying to forget. What else?"

I put on my kinetics and the shield formed around my head with a violet flash before fading away and becoming clear. Koda did the same and jumped on the Shroud.

"You may look old, but you actually have aim," she said grudgingly. "If this Night Warden thing doesn't work out, you could go into pest control."

"I already have my hands full in that department." I placed a hand on the Shroud. It rumbled to life and I slid into traffic. "Anything else?"

"The only other thing is that she didn't like your coat, but she kept mentioning it," she said, looking at my duster and pulling on one side of it. "I don't see what the big deal is. It's just a leather duster. Somewhat raggedy, if you ask me, but I do like the design. What is that, a mosquito?"

"I didn't *ask*, and you can see the design?" I asked surprised. Only one other person could see the dragonfly emblem on the back of my duster—Jade. The design was only visible to practitioners of a specific kind of magic. This was beginning to make sense. "Tessa would kill to get this coat. It was created by Aria."

No response.

"The Wordweaver?" I added. "Aria of the Wordweavers? The most powerful runecasters on the face of the Earth?"

"And what, that makes it a collectible?"

"This coat cost a fortune and a favor." I cut off a taxicab who shared some colorful words with me. "It's one of a kind."

"So you wear it for sentimental reasons?"

"There are two reasons I wear this coat," I answered with a sigh. "It's runed to the point that it's stronger than Kevlar and Dragonscale combined, which is especially useful since I'm not bulletproof or immune to large bursts of flame, and pockets that allow me to carry everything I need."

"Does this Aria make leathers?" Koda replied after a pause. "I'm not really the trench coat type."

"Doubt you could afford it. Owing a wordweaver a favor is no light matter, but you can ask." I shifted to one side to avoid traffic. "What else did you notice?"

I felt her shrug. "She didn't seem to know much about the LIT rounds or Redrum."

"Incorrect," I said, turning onto 1st Avenue, heading south. "She knows what's going on with this new strain of Redrum, but something has her spooked."

"I thought you said she's dangerous?"

"She is. Which means?"

Silence for a few more seconds. "Whatever or whoever has her scared is even more dangerous."

I nodded. "Maybe there's hope for you." I turned onto the FDR and sped downtown.

We arrived at The Dive. It had avoided the wave of gentrification to hit the area a few years back, because I was able to buy the entire building. The building itself was a converted carriage house with the bar on the ground floor and my apartment on the top two levels.

I'd sunk a small fortune in the interior restoration and runework. The runes were strong enough to make The Dive a fortress if I needed it to be.

"What's this place?" Koda asked as I parked the bike. "Is this where you live?"

"It's where *we* live—yes."

She looked around with a grunt of disapproval. "What's this look, 'modern ghetto'?"

"It looks better on the inside." I got off the Shroud and headed inside. "Let's go. I need to contact one of my sources."

"I hope this source works with the Buildings Department and this place is slated for demolition," she said as we crossed the threshold.

The runes on the doorframe hummed as we entered, and I could feel the dampening effect as we entered the building. Inside was a mixture of mahogany and cherry woods. The floor was red marble. Every surface was runed, creating a magic vacuum.

Cole stood behind the large wooden bar and nodded as I came in. He wore his usual black T-shirt and jeans ensemble. Even though it looked like he lived in the gym, I'd never seen him outside of The Dive for longer than an hour. I asked him about it once. He gave me his usual wordy answer. Genetics."

Foy Vance's gravelly voice came over the sound system, imploring for rain as we approached the bar. The bittersweet feel of the music complemented the mix of honey and lemon I sensed every time I stepped into The Dive.

"What fresh hell is this?" Frank said from the corner of the bar. "You picking up strays from the street now,

Grey?"

"That thing can talk?" Koda asked as she squinted in the dim light. "Is that a lizard?"

"Shit," I muttered under my breath. "He doesn't like being called a—"

"Lizard?" Frank hissed and stalked closer to Koda. "Did she just call me a *lizard*?"

"Well, technically, it's what you are," I said, trying to head off the explosion. "It was an honest mistake, she didn't—"

"Shut it," Frank said while holding up a leg and pointing at me. Small arcs of electricity jumped off his body. He turned to face Koda. "The correct term is *dragon*. Miss...?"

"Koda," she said with a smile and reached over to pet Frank. I grabbed her hand before she made a fatal mistake. "What? He's cute."

"You don't want to do that—ever."

Koda pulled her hand back and moved down the bar. "What is he?"

"This one's sharp as a brick, Grey," Frank said, glaring at Koda. "I told you. I'm a dragon."

"He's a pain in my ass, is what he is." I slid Frank down to the other end of the bar. "I need to show her where she's staying. Think you can stay calm for five minutes?"

"She's staying here?" Frank flicked his tail in displeasure. "I thought you said you weren't going to —?"

"I know what I said. She's staying here. Can you behave?"

"Behave? Never." I stared at him. "Fine, I'll leave her

alone. Unless she calls me a lizard again. Then all bets are off. It'll be the end for *Miss Koda*."

"I saw what you did there," I said with a smile. "Not bad."

"Not bad?" Frank gave a mock bow. "I am a master."

"I need to find Street," I said as I pushed off the bar. "Find him."

"I think you mean, 'Find him, *please*, oh, great and fearful dragon of immense power.'"

"No, I meant find him—*now*, oh, small and puny lizard of questionable power, filled with delusions of grandeur."

Frank nodded, gave me two one-fingered salutes and circled in place with closed eyes. I motioned silently for Koda to follow me upstairs.

"Don't call him a lizard," I said when she caught up. "His name is Frank, but it's better if you just ignore him. Let me show you where you'll be staying."

The level above the bar was the training floor and library. Above that were the living quarters. I took her down to the south end and pointed to the door.

"This is you," I said with a nod. "I'll have Cole bring up the stuff Corbel dropped off so you can get settled. I'm at the other end. Don't go down there unless I tell you."

"Why not?" she asked, craning her neck around me and looking down the hallway. "What's down there?"

"My room, which is off limits." I looked at her and shook my head. "I prefer my privacy *not* be invaded, and the runes along the floor will blow you to bits if I don't deactivate them first. Downstairs in twenty."

I deactivated the runes because I knew she would try them at some point. I didn't want to scrape her off the walls and rebuild the top-half of the building. Her door opened and closed behind me and I glanced down the hallway. Nothing good would come of this.

I opened my door and another set of runes thrummed as I entered my room. It was twice the size of the entire third floor. I'd cheated by using the same runes that made the pockets of my coat larger than they actually were. I removed the case of ammunition and placed it on my worktable.

I took a moment to take a deep breath. I grabbed a pair of pruning shears and gave one of the closest bonsai some attention. I started growing them a few years back and initially had them all over The Dive, until Frank started setting them on fire. I moved them all into my room after that and left a select few downstairs as centerpieces for the dining tables.

Next to the table, in the center of the work area, I had etched a large circle into the wooden floor. I reached in and removed the sword Hades had given me. It jumped in my hand again. I placed the sword in the center of the circle and it hovered a few feet above the ground. I stepped back and touched the edge of the circle.

The runes around the outer edge flashed orange for a few seconds and then became dim. They pulsed every few seconds, and I knew the sword was secure. I wasn't going to become the host to some insane sword just because Hades wanted me to, even if it could stop the spell that was killing me.

The smell of chlorine filled the room, followed by

an electric charge that made the hairs on the back of my neck stand on end. The high-pitched sound of a triangle filled the room a second later.

"What is it?" I said without turning around. "Didn't I ask you to find Street? Don't burn my plants."

"You want the bad news or the worse news?" Frank said as he sat on the worktable and took a deep breath. "The air is always so fresh in the Stryder jungle."

"You know I hate it when you do that." I adjusted the runes around the circle holding the sword. Another orange flash let me know that a second layer of security surrounded the sword.

"Have you seen my legs?" he said, lifting one and wagging it at me. "You expect me to take the stairs?"

"Send Cole next time." I looked down at him and scowled. "Now it smells like a rancid swimming pool in here, and my ears are ringing, thanks."

"My pleasure," he said with a flourish. "Which is it?"

"Bad news first." I adjusted Fatebringer as he ported to my storage trunk with a crackle of energy.

"Several packs of rummers are loose on the streets," Frank said and spat. On the trunk. My ancient ironwood trunk that contained volatile magical items. Scorch marks formed where the saliva landed. "Shit, sorry."

I stared at him.

"It's the middle of the day." I grabbed a rune-covered cloth and threw it on the saliva, absorbing it. Last thing I needed was a magical fire. "NYTF or Dark Council taking action?"

"The usual—deflection and plausible deniability."

"So they aren't doing anything."

Frank nodded.

"Night Wardens?"

"You just said it." Frank shook his head. "It's the middle of the day and they're *Night* Wardens. They seem to take the title seriously."

"Which leaves—?" I said, knowing and hating the answer.

"Grey Stryder, rogue day *and* Night Warden, hero extraordinaire," Frank said with a bow. "Keeping the streets of our fair city safe from the menace of the night. Speaking of menace—why is there an angry dark blade in your room?"

"I'm holding it for someone," I said. "It's going back ASAP."

"Good, it's giving off some serious dark mojo." He looked down and twitched his tail anxiously. "The kind that makes me want to wet myself. I would hate to ruin your nice trunk."

"Don't make me squash you." I raised a hand menacingly. "What's the worse news?"

"Those rummers? They're closing in on Street's last position."

"What? Fuck! Why didn't you tell me that first?"

"I asked you what you wanted to hear first—*you* said the bad news."

I glared at him. "Go get Koda and meet me downstairs. Now."

"Really?" Frank shook his body, sending small electric sparks in every direction. "Are you sure?"

"Don't give her a heart attack." I grabbed two more speed loaders and my coat and headed out of the room.

EIGHT

I HEARD THE screaming followed by cursing as I raced downstairs. Cole was behind the bar. Frank materialized with a small thunderclap a few seconds later.

"Thank you for that, Grey," Frank said with what passed for a grin. "She'll be down right away."

"Where is he?" I kept my voice calm, but my stomach was in a knot. "Can you pinpoint Street?"

"He's moving around too much," Frank answered. "It's hard to get an exact location."

I'd be moving around if I had a pack of rummers on my ass too. *Why would they be after Street?*

"How do you know it's rummers? Could just be runic interference?" I said, hoping against hope. "Maybe it's a Ziller wave?"

Frank stared at me as if I had hit my head repeatedly.

"Ziller waves would boost his signature, not obscure it," Frank replied. "This is reading wrong, twisted—like a rummer. Lots of them."

"Damn it," I said under my breath. "I need a

location. Frank, give me a general area."

I stepped back as Frank turned in a circle on the bar. I learned early on that it was better to stand back when he was doing his location thing.

"Best I can give you is Central Park, south end, near Columbus Circle." Frank shook his head and small arcs of electrical energy leaped off him. "You'd better get moving. Is short and sassy upstairs any good at fighting?"

"Worked for Hades, as a cleaner of some kind," I said, checking Fatebringer. I reached under the bar for three more speed loaders with LIT rounds, putting them in a pocket. I kept ammunition stashed throughout The Dive. Better to have it and not need it than the alternative.

Frank spat on the bar.

"You realize that's disgusting, right?" I said, looking at him and throwing another runed towel on the saliva. "At least use the sink or don't do that at all."

"What's disgusting is your vetting process," Frank said, squinting at me. "She could be a spy *for* Hades for all you know."

"I don't think Hades is too concerned with one ex-Night Warden."

"You think it's a coincidence he picked you?" Frank scoffed. "He knows you. Better than you know yourself."

"Doesn't matter," I snapped back. "She stays."

"This is the same thing you did with Jade. You went off without checking and—"

He stopped when he saw my expression.

"This is *nothing* like that," I said, my voice steel.

"Koda works with me or Hades retires her. That simple."

"It's never *that* simple with gods, there's always a cost," Frank stared at me. "Let him retire her, Grey."

"No," I said, ending the conversation as Koda came downstairs. "She stays until I say otherwise."

"If your horny lizard sneaks into my room again, I'm going to cut first and ask questions never." Koda glared at Frank and then turned to me. "Did you send him?"

"Me? Why would I send him?" I feigned offense and stared at Frank. "He's uncontrollable."

"Hello, Kitty." Frank waved a leg and tried to suppress a chuckle. "Didn't realize you were a cat person—nice underwear."

A fan sliced through the air where Frank had been standing a half-second earlier. It arced across the bar and returned to Koda's hand, leaving a trail of red energy in its wake.

Frank reappeared at the end of the bar, spat, and turned to Cole. "Cole, pour me a drink. My delicate nerves can barely take the menace from fangirl." Frank pointed at me. "At least she can keep you cool if things get hot, Grey."

"You're dead, *lizard*," Koda hissed as she burst out of The Dive, kicking the door open and cursing.

NINE

"I THINK FRANK likes you." I placed a hand on the Shroud and the engine roared to life before settling into a rumbling purr. "It usually takes a few days before someone tries to kill him."

"Your lizard is a freak." She put on her kinetics and jumped behind me on the Shroud. "What the hell is his problem?"

"Few things you should know about Frank," I said with a sigh. "He's touchy, angry, and ill-tempered."

"Like his owner?"

I shook my head. "I don't *own* Frank—no one does. He just showed up one day."

"Then what the hell is he?" she asked, calming down. "Lizards don't usually speak."

"As far as anyone knows, Frank was a mage," I said, starting the Shroud. "A powerful one who screwed up a transmutation spell. Which is how he ended up trapped in that body."

"He must not have been very good," she muttered under her breath. "What was he trying to turn into?"

"A dragon," I said as I rode off the sidewalk and sped down the street. "A real one."

"Serves him right," she muttered. She reflexively held on as I picked up speed. "Where's the fire?"

"Central Park, rummers are after my source."

"Rummers? It's the middle of the day," Koda said and squeezed my abdomen as I cut a corner and jumped a curb. I sped up the FDR Drive and weaved through traffic. "They must be the new and improved versions if they aren't bursting all over the place."

"How good are you with those fans?" I asked as I cut through traffic. "Tell me you can actually hit something with them."

"I'm decent," she said. "Not at my grandfather's level, but I can hold my own."

"We're facing rummers. You need to be better than decent." I turned off the FDR at the 63rd Street exit and raced across the city. "I told Hades the only ass I cover is my own. You get yourself ghosted, it's on you."

"Good to know you have my back in case something goes sideways."

"Have your back?" I said incredulously. "When it gets real and your next breath may be your last—you're alone. No one has your back."

"Weren't you part of the Night Wardens?" she asked. "Didn't they have your back? Didn't you trust them?"

"I'll tell you what I trust," I said, holding the memories back and keeping the rage out of my voice. "I trust my eye, my gun, and my bullets. If you want to survive on these streets more than one night, trust no one. Not even me, understand?"

Silence. She shifted in the seat and looked over my right shoulder. "I'm just trying to figure out which one got you kicked out of the Night Wardens, the winning personality or the warm cuddly friendliness?"

"Neither," I said, turning into Columbus Circle. "I left them after they forced me to kill my partner."

This time I expected the silence. The image of Jade's twisted body rushed at me as we entered under the canopy of trees. She used to love Central Park. The moment of her death crept up and replayed itself in my mind, opening up old wounds and pouring in ample doses of salt.

Lyrra's words whispered in my ear again.

You have to do it, Grey. The spell is out of control and will kill us all if you don't. She needs to die and you're the only one who can get close enough.

"Stryder, where are all the people?" The undercurrent of fear in Koda's voice brought me back. "The park is never this empty."

"Mantis shrimp," I said, looking around. I let my senses expand and felt a tremor of activity on the fringes of my range ahead of us. "Ever hear of it?"

"Mantis shrimp? What, are you hungry?"

"Magic-users are like the shrimp." I turned off the engine and coasted for a few feet before getting off the Shroud and parking it. "Mantis shrimp can see twelve colors, while humans can only see three. Magic-users can see in a runispectral wavelength once our abilities manifest."

"That doesn't explain why the park is empty," she said and flicked her wrists with a gesture. The fans materialized in her hands a second later. "That just explains why we can see supernatural creatures and normals can't."

I stopped and felt for the latent runic signatures in the area. Street had been through here, with a larger signature overlapping his. This tracking ability is what made the Wardens dangerous. All I needed was the faintest runic signature and I could locate anyone given enough time.

"When do normals see past the veil and into the runispectral wavelengths?" I unholstered Fatebringer and picked up my pace. "When do they see the creatures?"

"When they feel intense fear," Koda answered. "I've had targets see through my camouflage because of the fear response."

I nodded and signaled for her to stop behind some trees. At the edge of the Great Lawn, I saw a man running in our direction. Close behind him, a group of ten rummers followed.

"The cortisol, adrenaline, and glucose cocktail allows them to see past the veil," I said, slowing my breathing. "On some level their limbic system is picking up a threat. That's why the park is empty—everyone left."

Koda nodded and closed her eyes. She said some words under her breath and her fans glowed bright orange-red for a few seconds, resembling hot lava. The magic wasn't strong enough to fire on my auditory senses but I sensed its presence as she spoke.

I took aim and fired. One of the group dropped, but got to its feet seconds later and resumed the chase. "So much for LIT rounds." I pulled out a speed loader and emptied Fatebringer into my palm, switching out for negation rounds. "Street!" I yelled. "This way."

"Do we take any of them alive?" Koda asked as we moved into position. "Perhaps a sample of the blood?"

I shook my head as the man looked in my direction and ran at me. "Cut first and cut fast," I said as they approached. "Rummers will shred you if you let them. Don't let them. We can get blood afterward if we really need it."

Koda took a defensive stance and opened both fans. The sound was a *thwump* followed by a metallic ring. Red energy cascaded from them as she outstretched both arms releasing the fans.

I realized two things as the fans decapitated two rummers and circled back to Koda, decapitating two more on the return trip: Her fans were dangerous weapons in the right hands, and there were a lot more than ten rummers headed our way.

Street turned on his heel and joined his hands together. Black tendrils shot out from his fingers, impaling five rummers and disintegrating them on impact. I shot the last rummer as the larger group came into view. It was easily three times the size of the first group.

"That—is a lot of rummers," Koda said backing up. "Unless you have a machine gun in that coat, we need to get out of here in a hurry."

"Get Street to the Shroud," I said, heading toward the rummers. "Get out of the park. I'll meet you at The Dive."

"You can't take on all those rummers alone." Koda stood her ground. "Are you insane?"

"I don't intend to," I said. "Now go!"

I cut across the pack of rummers and fired into the throng, and they diverted their attention to the immediate threat. In the distance, I heard the engine of the Shroud roar to life and diminish as they left the park.

I ran on the lawn with the pack after me. I had a few questions for Street, but first I had to survive a mindless mob of hungry vampires.

TEN

I HOLSTERED FATEBRINGER. I needed both hands free if this was going to work. I didn't relish the pain, but it was the only way to get rid of the rummer mob without endangering the normals in the area. I put some distance between us and managed to get behind one of the large boulders that dotted the landscape of the park.

Casting was my only option.

They had my runic scent now and I could hear them closing in on my location. I needed them to get close for this to work.

The energy flowed through me. The pain was immediate and blinding. I went down on one knee to catch my breath as the mob approached. Most of them were dressed in rags and torn clothing. Their glowing red eyes, bright even in the afternoon, only saw one thing when they focused on me: their next meal.

I gestured and my blood turned to acid in my veins, burning everything. I clenched my teeth to block out the pain and managed to finish the rune. Black tendrils erupted from the grass and impaled the rummers in place. Their howls of pain filled the afternoon, followed by my grunt of bone-crushing agony.

Holding them in place was the first phase of the spell. I needed to finish before the pain overwhelmed me and they got free. I began tracing the second set of runes, when the sound of foghorns filled the park. Someone was casting something large and nasty.

Sweat poured into my eyes and the ground swayed for a moment as I paused to catch my breath again. I spat out blood and began to trace the runes again. I felt a surge of energy wash over the area. The tendrils disappeared.

"Shit," I said and drew Fatebringer. I formed a black orb of energy and released it into the center of the rummers as I started firing. The explosion of negative energy scattered them as I dropped a few more with negation rounds.

A rummer broke away from the pack and leaped at me. I turned, "ready to introduce it to my boot", when its head flew off, causing the body to burst into dust.

"What the—?" I looked around and saw a few more become instant dust clouds. "I thought I told you to get Street out of the park?"

"I did get him out of the park," she said, ducking under several swipes and slashing with one fan as she released the other, dusting several of the rummers that were advancing on our position. "Now I'm here to get you out of the park."

"I have this handled," I said with a growl as I fired and erased another group of the mindless vampires. "I don't need help."

The pain behind my eyes throbbed and my grip on Fatebringer was shaky at best. I was glad to see her, even though I said otherwise. I didn't look forward to being torn to pieces by the rummers, which would have been the outcome if she hadn't disobeyed me.

"Of course you do," Koda said, catching a fan and removing the arm of a rummer who had been about to slash at her. "This looks completely handled."

A surge of energy thrummed against my senses. More rummers were coming.

"Where did you leave the Shroud?" In a few minutes, we were going to be overrun. "We have more rummers coming."

"More?" she said, jumping back and rolling away from a group of rummers intent on making her a snack. I fired and dropped three more. "How many more?"

"Too many for us to deal with, without attracting major attention," I said as I speed loaded another seven rounds. "We need to bail or we'll become lunch."

Koda backflipped away from another swipe and clambered over the boulder behind me. "This way."

I glanced up at her, shook my head, and fired an orb of air at the ground. It launched me over the boulder. I landed on my ass on the other side as the rummers screamed in frustration. A few feet away, Koda started the Shroud and I jumped on, leaving the mob of angry vampires behind us.

"How the hell did you start—?"

"Whoever did your runic defenses needs to brush up on security," she said, racing out of the park. "These were easier than the ones on your pistol."

"You and I are going to have a talk about personal boundaries."

"We could always go back, and I could drop you off with the angry vamps?" she said, and I could hear the smile. "Which, by the way, aren't leaving the park because—?"

"Because they're being controlled by something or someone."

"That doesn't sound good," she said. "Who needs to control rummers?"

"That's the right question." I turned back and saw the rummers running in the opposite direction and dispersing. "I'm going to have to make some calls."

She handled the Shroud with ease—not that I would ever tell her that. That was twice that she had bypassed defenses meant to incapacitate or kill without a second thought. She was dangerous and lethal. I needed to speak to Corbel, but first things first.

"Where's Street?" She swerved expertly between two benches as we left the park. "Tell me you didn't leave him somewhere in the park."

"Over there." She pointed with her chin. "Old guy looks in bad shape."

"Show some respect," I said, motioning to him. "He's older than both of us combined and has more power in one finger than you have in your entire body."

"Why didn't he erase the rummers then?" she asked indignantly. "Would've saved us a lot of trouble."

"Having power isn't the same as being able to use it," I answered. "He went through a rough patch a few years back. Fried him. He doesn't remember much of who he was. He casts on instinct now."

"*This* is your source—some half-baked mage firing on three cylinders?"

"Street isn't just my source, he's my friend," I said, keeping my anger in check. "Do not insult him."

"Got it. Be nice to the senior citizen."

"Nothing happens on the street without his knowing about it—that's how he earned his name," I growled at her. "If he says something is going down, it's as good as done."

On the other side of Columbus Circle stood Street, fidgeting and looking nervous. He wore an old coat over an old threadbare shirt and worn-out pants. Everything about his appearance seemed old, except his socks and boots. I always made sure to get him a new pair when they wore out. That and food were the only things he would accept from me.

He pulled his long gray hair into a ponytail as I approached, but he never took his eyes off the park entrance.

"Eyes and ears open, mouth closed," I said as Koda parked the Shroud in front of Masa, a Dark Council neutral zone. "He doesn't like strangers and they don't come stranger than you right now."

"I've got nothing to say to the old mage whose life I just saved," she said. "*Or* to his deranged friend who is currently batshit crazy."

I glared at her, and she raised her hands in surrender. I felt her shadowing me silently as I walked over to the old mage and put a hand on his shoulder.

"Thanks, Grey," Street said as I started walking away from Masa. The last thing I needed was the Dark Council on my ass about a bunch of angry vamps running around the Park. "You saved me in there."

"How're you feeling, Street?" I waved his words away. "You getting enough to eat? Ezra says he isn't seeing you downtown much these days."

"I like the other guy—Pieri, or is it Piero? Memory isn't what it used to be," Street answered. "His food is always good and he's closer. He's nice to me."

"Did Ezra say something?" I asked, concerned. "He can be a bit odd, but he's good people."

"No no no," Street answered quickly, shaking his head. "His food is good too—real good, especially the sandwiches, but something about him feels wrong, so I go to Pieri's. He's *only* a vampire. Ezra is more than a vampire...cold. He scares me deep in my bones."

I was certain Ezra got that reaction often. Piero Roselli owned several restaurants around the city. I'd made sure Street was welcome at any of his establishments after resolving a delicate situation for Piero a few years ago.

"Besides, Ezra is too far, too far," Street said patting down his coat. "Have something for you. They were my friends, Grey. Now they're wrong, all wrong."

He handed me a vial with a dark liquid. I knew what it was without having to open it—Redrum.

"Where did you get this?"

"They forced them to drink it, Grey. The blackboots," Street said, looking around. "Turned my friends all wrong. I have to go. Need to get safe. They're after me."

I wasn't going to get any information from him in this state. Stress flipped him from lucid to deranged paranoia. It didn't get more stressful than being chased by a pack of rummers, or whoever he felt the 'blackboots' were.

"Street," I said, grabbing his arm when he wouldn't look at me, "I need you to stay out of the park. Can you do that?"

"Park's not safe—time to go underground," Street muttered more to himself. "Underground, I'll be safe."

I let him go and made sure he went into the subway system. He would disappear down there for few days, but he would be safe. Once he regained some sense of self, he would reach out and we would meet. Until then, I needed to go see Aria and have a conversation with a certain Hound.

ELEVEN

I HANDED THE vial to Koda.

"What do you see?"

She turned it over in her hand. It was small and cylindrically shaped, with a large stopper on one end. The iridescent liquid glimmered as she turned it.

"Redrum?" she said, unsure. "How bad is this?"

"Imagine a drug that gives you the abilities of a vampire and is more addictive than heroin, without any of the downsides." I took the vial from her hand. "The first dose is all power—you're faster, stronger, and all your reflexes are off the charts."

"Those things in the park weren't on their first dose." She looked across the street at the entrance to the park and shuddered. "And what the hell happened to their eyes?"

"The drug breaks down and destroys melanin in the body. Iris color, skin pigmentation... eventually they lose all color."

"That's why they can't handle UV radiation?"

I held up the Redrum. "That's the mutation of the

drug. But I'm sure that's part of it," I said, putting the vial in a pocket. "What else did you notice?"

"Are you talking before or after I saved your ass?" she said with a smirk. "Sorry, I mean while you were 'handling' things."

"Before, when I had the rummers impaled." I pulled out my phone as we headed back to the Shroud.

"I felt a surge," she said. "And then all hell broke loose. That's when I had to save—I mean help—you handle the rummers."

"I need you to take the bike to The Dive and wait there for me," I said, looking at her. "Do you think you can do that?"

"Are you planning to go back in there?" She looked at the park again and crossed her arms. "If you are, I'm staying."

"No, at least not without an army of backup." She gave me a hard stare, which I'm sure worked on most. I was immune to her scolding glare. At my age, too many life-ending monsters had turned my blood to ice with their glares. It made her attempt at intimidation pale in comparison. "You keep staring at me like that, I know a spell that will keep your face stuck in that expression."

She started the Shroud and grinned at my reaction.

"Told you, the security runes were craptastic." The engine settled into a low rumble. "I'm serious, Stryder. Stay out of there. Whole place creeps me the hell out."

"I'll be down in a few hours and we can go see Aria about the Redrum," I said, walking off. "Make sure you don't total the bike. It's not exactly cheap, Cecil would be pissed if he had to replace it."

This was a test on several levels. Would she go to The Dive, or disobey and attempt to follow me? I watched her roar off and head down Broadway. I pressed a button on my phone. The call connected on the second ring.

"Where?" the voice said.

"Lincoln Center Fountain," I said, looking around. "Thirty minutes."

"That pretty public."

"The last time I wanted to meet in private, I was attacked by several armed men and a renegade mage."

"It's a dangerous city."

"I'm one of the reasons it is," I said. "Don't be late." I disconnected the call and headed up Broadway. The Hound of Hades had some explaining to do.

TWELVE

LINCOLN CENTER WAS a bustling plaza of activity, especially in the middle of the afternoon. I let my senses expand outward. I sensed a few magic-users in the vicinity, but nothing concentrated enough to indicate an intent to surround me.

I approached the fountain and closed my eyes for several seconds. Corbel was nearby. I sensed him before I saw him, standing on the far end of the fountain.

"I don't know why they called you dragonfly," Corbel said when I approached. "You're more of a hound than I ever was."

"No one calls me that anymore."

"No one who's still living, you mean," he answered and I wanted to punch him in the face for mentioning Jade—even indirectly. "I'm sorry. That was callous."

He wanted a reaction. I gave him one—indifference.

"I'm dealing with a volatile situation so I would appreciate you being straight with me," I said without looking at him. "What is she?"

"Important," he answered after a brief pause.

"To whom?"

"Me, Hades, and you."

"I work alone and like it that way."

"Good thing you weren't alone this afternoon," he said. "Yes, I'm keeping tabs on *her*."

"So that whole line about retiring her was—?"

"Just enough to get you to agree," he answered. "He knows you. We all know you, Stryder. Diamond on the outside, cotton on the inside. It's what makes you predictable—"

"And dangerous," I finished. "You didn't answer my question."

I didn't enjoy being played by anyone, especially not by gods and their minions. I was going to have to jerk the Hound's leash tight to get a real answer.

"I can't," he said with a sigh. "It would defeat the purpose of having her with you. I'm not the only one keeping tabs on her and *you*."

I had enough enemies to make the obvious question pointless.

"So I have to keep Kano's granddaughter safe and sound, while not knowing the extent of her abilities?"

He visibly paled at my words. "How did you get that information?" he said. "There's no proof that she's related to—"

"Of course there isn't," I said, keeping track of the plaza with my senses. "That's the point. Doesn't mean it isn't true."

"Grey," he said slowly, "very few people know about that incident."

"I don't like playing games, Corbel." I turned and

looked into the spraying water of the fountain. "Either you tell me who and what she is, or I go see your boss and have a conversation with him. And by *conversation*, I mean kick his divine ass all over his office."

"Are you insane?" Corbel asked. "You can't face him and survive."

I held up my index and middle fingers. "Two things: one, I'm dying anyway so I have nothing to lose"—I curled my index finger, leaving my middle finger up —"and two, there's a brand-new shiny sword in my place that says I can."

"Stryder, you're powerful, but not *that* powerful, even with the sword," he said, looking at me now and scowling. "Have you grown tired of breathing?"

The words lacked conviction, and I turned to face him. "You're wasting my time," I said, stepping away from the fountain.

"Wait," he said as he looked around. "Not here. Too many ears."

This was uncharacteristic for Corbel, who usually didn't care about being overheard. It meant the information was sensitive—and dangerous.

"Where?" I asked cautiously. If he suggested one of Hades' properties, I'd find out another way. I wasn't walking into another ambush.

"Roselli's on 23rd, the one on the roof."

"Flat Earth?"

He nodded. "They have state-of-the-art runic security after the ogre incident. Plus the food is excellent."

Flat Earth had been renovated a few years back after an ogre rampaged through the place, tearing it to shreds. I heard it had something to do with Simon and Tristan. Those two had a reputation for massive destruction wherever they went. I was surprised the city was still standing after their exploits.

"Two days," he said. "Give me two days, and then I'll tell you what you need to know."

"No," I said. "Two days, and you'll tell me what I *want* to know. She can see my dragonfly. Only Jade saw my dragonfly, Aria designed it that way. That tells me several things."

"Shit," he muttered. "She's stronger than I imagined. Two days—give me that much time."

I gave him a short nod. "I'm speaking to your boss on day three if you don't show."

He stepped away from the fountain and lost himself in the crowd. I tried to sense him, but he was gone. I made a mental note about his masking ability. It was my experience that acquaintances can easily turn into adversaries.

I put on my kinetics and adjusted the communicator.

"You there?" I asked and waited. The range was excellent but it wasn't infinite. In the background, I could hear glass breaking and knew Koda had made it to The Dive.

"What?" Koda asked, clearly upset. "Do you really need your lizard—yes, I said *lizard*—alive?"

"Leave Frank alone."

"Excuse me?" she hissed, her voice ice. "Did you just ask *me* to leave *him* alone?"

Frank was going to get me killed one day. "Listen, I need you to step outside and get some air."

"Can't at the moment," she whispered. "Someone

just came in—fried all your runes at the door. Your security truly sucks. He's looking for the Dragonfly and he seems pissed."

"Describe him."

"Tall, dark skin, darker attitude, wearing some kind of black uniform, and pretty intimidating."

"Is he alone?"

"No, two more with him, females—twins, and they look dangerous too," Koda said. "You know this Dragonfly person they're looking for?"

"Yes, I do."

"Who are these people?" she asked. "I'm not getting the regular patron vibe from them."

"I'm on my way," I said, keeping the concern from my voice. "Whatever you do, don't engage them. Just sit tight."

"Sure. And who am I not engaging?"

"You're looking at Quinton and the Twins."

I groaned when I said it, knowing what the response would be.

"Are you serious? Do they go on tour too?"

"Shut it," I hissed. "They're Night Wardens and dangerous. Keep your fans hidden and don't say a word. I'm on my way."

Quinton and the Twins were a Night Warden assassination team, but Koda was right. They rarely conducted business during the day. If he was at The Dive with the Twins—I could never tell them apart, so I started calling them Thing One and Thing Two—the options were limited. By sending them, the Night Wardens wanted to send me a message. 'Stop or we'll stop you—permanently.' Now I just had to find out what they wanted me to stop doing.

THIRTEEN

I HEADED DOWN into the subway.

There was only one way I would get there fast enough. I needed a Transporter.

Transporters were magic-users with one specific ability: they were master teleporters. No mage could match a transporter's speed or level of precision. After my run-in with the rummers earlier, I didn't trust myself to try casting again without passing out from the pain.

There was only one problem. Transporters needed to 'read' your runic signature before they would shift you where you wanted to go. Your deepest emotions would be exposed and raw. It was about as pleasant as it sounded.

I let my senses expand and felt out the station. My range was much shorter underground, at most eighty meters or so if I pushed it. I jumped down off the platform and walked farther into the tracks. Every station usually had one Transporter, you just had to know where to find them.

Sometimes they lurked on the platforms, but most often, they stayed on the tracks between stations. The larger stations like Penn or Grand Central had about a dozen, strategically situated throughout the station to handle the flow of teleportation. The subtly sweet sensation hit me before I felt her energy signature between stations. I approached slowly. They didn't like to be startled.

I saw her huddled against the wall. She smiled when she saw me and waved me closer. Every Transporter looked the same—an old woman wrapped in too many layers. It was the perfect camouflage in the city. I was never able to determine what race they belonged to. I just knew they weren't human.

"Hello, grandmother," I said as I stepped closer. "I need a shift."

"Do you now?" She stretched out her hand. I crouched down and winced, placing my hand in hers. She shook her head, tutting at me. "You've been messing about with darkness, haven't you?"

"Long ago, yes."

She shook her head again and looked up at me. "You need to let her go, my child," she said. "No good will come of holding her in your heart like this."

"I have." I pulled my hand gently out of hers.

She wagged her finger at me and narrowed her eyes.

"You can lie to yourself, but not to me," she said, standing. "Where do you need to go?"

I told her the address of The Dive. "Just outside please."

She nodded. "Do you have something for me?" she asked expectantly.

I reached in my pocket and pulled out two squares of Godiva dark chocolate I kept for just these occasions. Transporters didn't accept money as payment. A trinket of some kind it would work, but they preferred chocolate.

"Will this do?" I extended the squares, and she snatched them faster than I could track.

She nearly squealed in delight and then grew serious with a short cough. "Yes, that will be adequate," she said with a large smile. She spread her hands apart, and a large runic circle formed under my feet. It transitioned from red to green to blue in a loop of bright colors. "Are you prepared?"

I nodded. A transporter shift violated most of Ziller's known laws of time and space. Rather than teleporting you where you wanted to go, it warped time, space, and gravity around you so that the place you wanted to go aligned to your location.

When you were aligned, the Transporter would give you the equivalent of a runic kick and send you down the bridge she created. No mage in history has been able to teleport using this method.

You ended up where you wanted—in one piece, but a bit worn out. The way you would feel after a hard sprint. Since I couldn't cast, I didn't have much of a choice. I closed my eyes and felt the world tilt sideways.

FOURTEEN

I ARRIVED ACROSS the street from The Dive a few seconds later. It took me a few moments to catch my breath before I could examine the runic defenses and realized Koda was right. Quinton blew right through them. I needed better security. Right now, I had to deal with three assassins in my home.

If I walked in with Fatebringer drawn, Quinton would shoot first and ask my perforated body questions later. I opted for diplomacy. If it were an erasure, Cole, Frank, and Koda would be corpses and The Dive would be engulfed in flames by now.

I didn't smell smoke. The odds of everyone still being alive were good. I walked around to the side of the building and placed my hand on several bricks in a specific sequence.

This opened a stairwell to the second floor. I went to my room, activated the failsafe runes, and placed the vial Street had given me on the worktable. Any magic cast in the building now would fry the caster, causing horrific pain followed by unconsciousness. I hoped that by blasting through my security, Quinton would assume the defenses were still down.

I walked downstairs and took in the scene.

Cole stood behind the bar, with Frank on the end farthest from the door. Koda sat on a stool in the center of the bar. One of the twins stood by the door, the other stood at the foot of the stairs, blocking them. Quinton sat at one of the tables in the center of the floor, nursing a drink.

"Excuse me," I said, causing the twin blocking the stairs to jump and growl at me as she drew her blades. "Hello, Quinton."

Quinton looked at her and she resheathed her weapons, cursing under her breath.

"Dragonfly," he said as he kicked out a chair for me. I walked over to the bar. "We need to talk."

"Painkiller, Cole."

"Isn't it a little early for that?" Cole said, grabbing the bottle of vodka. "How about a coffee?"

"Transporter equals Painkiller," I said with a grunt as he poured the five shots of vodka into a pint of stout. My condition made intoxication impossible, but the mix of alcohol calmed down the after-effects of the shift. He placed the drink in front of me with a disapproving stare.

"You're the Dragonfly?" Koda asked, surprised.

"No one calls me that anymore." I looked at Quinton. "How can I help you?"

I sat at the table and made sure I had access to Fatebringer as I sipped my drink. The centerpiece was one of the few bonsai I'd left on the ground floor.

"You're looking good for a dead man." He grabbed a

branch and snapped it. "You're not still touchy about your shrubs, are you?"

"Just a plant."

"Maybe I should take up some gardening?" He snapped another branch. "It seems to be doing you well."

"Thank you. Clean eating, and clean living works wonders." I took another sip. The ambient magic was as bitter as my drink. The failsafes were designed to inflict mind-shattering pain. I really hoped he would try casting. "Are you here to get my secret?"

"I'm here to ask a question and give you some advice," he said and placed his hands on the table. Two immense hand cannons rested in them. "For old times' sake."

"I'm touched." I knew what he wanted. This wasn't a courtesy call. "Ask."

"Where's the old mage?"

"You over-estimate my abilities." I placed my glass on the table. "There are hundreds of old mages in this city."

"I'm only concerned with one—he goes by the name of Street."

"I've heard of him, but I don't keep tabs on all the mages in the city."

"My source says you keep close tabs on this one."

"Your source is wrong." I stared right into his eyes without flinching. "What did he do?"

"He took something that doesn't belong to him." Quinton narrowed his eyes at me. "I need it back."

"If I see him, I'll let him know that stealing is hazardous to his health."

"You do that." He shifted the hand cannons in his hands. "You want my advice, Dragonfly?"

"I can barely contain myself with the anticipation," I deadpanned. "Do share."

"Retire before you're retired," he said with a malicious grin. "Stop your patrols."

"Is that advice or a threat?" I looked down at the large guns. They were covered in dangerous-looking runes. "Those are some serious cannons."

"You like them?" He patted the sides of the two Marlin BFRs. They made Fatebringer look like a small pistol. "I call them 'Shock and Awe'."

"I call them compensating for being small somewhere else." I looked at him and raised an eyebrow. "Why do you need two of them?"

"For old mages who don't get the message the first time"—he held up one of the guns—"I have a follow-up." He held up the second gun. "For example, you're taking actions that'll get you ghosted violently."

Behind me, I felt the Twins tense up and shift their weight forward slightly to come up on the balls of their feet. This could go sideways in seconds. I took a deep breath and focused.

"Such as?" I asked innocently. "Last I heard, walking in the park wasn't against Night Warden rules. Have they changed that?"

"*You* aren't a Night Warden, Stryder, not anymore." He holstered his guns and I breathed a little easier. "Stop trying to hold onto the past. Your Warden days were done the day you killed your—"

I placed Fatebringer on the table faster than he could blink. He nodded as I felt the Twins behind me take a step in my direction. Quinton looked over at them, and they stayed where they were.

"I'm going to *advise* you not to go there, Quinton."

He stood and pushed his chair back.

"This is the only courtesy Lyrra is extending." He pulled on his coat and looked down at me. "Stay out of the park and stop hunting the rummers. I would hate to have to put you down, but I will."

"That *was* a lot of rummers in one place," I said, slowly. "Wonder how they all got their hands on Redrum?"

"That kind of wondering can get you killed, or worse, Dragonfly." Quinton leaned down and whispered into my ear, "You don't need to worry about a bunch of homeless people no one cares about anyway."

I clenched my jaw and refrained from firing Fatebringer into his face repeatedly.

"You tell Lyrra I said thank you for the courtesy. Now get the fuck out of my home."

Quinton's left eye twitched slightly. An old tic from our training days when he was stressed. He laughed but placed a hand on one of his holsters. "I always did like you, Dragonfly," he said and nodded to the Twins. They headed to the door and stepped outside. "But I won't think twice about ghosting your old ass. I expect not to see you on the streets."

"Don't worry, Q," I said without looking up at him. "If memory serves, you were always a bit slow on the uptake. You won't see me coming—until it's too late."

He gave me a small bow and left The Dive. I heard the roaring engine of a large vehicle, which grew fainter as it drove away. I placed my hand over the other one holding the Fatebringer to stop the small tremors.

Koda came over to the table. I holstered Fatebringer as I tried to calm my breathing. Last thing I needed was her being worried.

"Cole, call Java and tell him I need real runic defenses in here, or I'm going to rip off his arm and beat him silly with it." I downed the Painkiller. "Tell him I want him here before I go out tonight."

"Wait…what?" Koda asked, incredulously. "You're going out after that warning?"

"No, *we're* going out after that warning." I grabbed my phone. "We're going to need more than the Shroud though, if Lyrra unleashed Quinton and his girls."

"You're insane," Koda said with a small smile and sat at the table. "That human wall is looking for a reason to make you resemble Swiss cheese. Didn't you see those things he calls guns?"

"It's not the size of the pistol—but the steadiness of the hand holding it," I shot back. "Besides, it's not like I have a long future ahead of me."

"His hand looked plenty steady to me," she said, looking at me. "You sure this is a good idea?"

"Tell me what you learned," I said, ignoring her question.

"They have something to do with the rummers in the park."

I nodded. "Obviously. What else?"

"This Lyrra is scared of you or what you can do— she wants you off the streets and she sent tall, dark, and ugly with his bookends to let you know all bets are off if you go out."

"No one tells me to stay off the streets in my city—no one," I growled. "What else?"

She paused before speaking, which meant she was giving this one thought—a good sign.

"Between what he whispered and what Street said, they're forcing the homeless to take this new strain of Redrum," she said slowly, trying to gauge my reaction. "I just don't know why."

"Which is why we're going out tonight."

"Fine, I got your six. I'm sure we can get matching caskets."

"I'm feeling safer already." I dialed SuNaTran. "First, we need a better ride. The Shroud is too vulnerable."

"Can I keep the Shroud?" she asked, her voice full of hope.

"Absolutely—not."

She growled, giving me the stink-eye.

"SuNaTran," said the voice over the phone in a crisp English accent. "How can we meet your transportation needs?"

"Hello, Alice, I need the Beast," I said, looking at Koda. "And two subdermal communicators with extended range."

"The Beast, sir? Are you certain?" she said after a pause. "May I suggest a less volatile vehicle?"

"No, Alice, you may not," I said. "Clear it with Cecil."

"Please hold."

I glanced over at Cole, who was shaking his head.

"What?" I asked. "Stop being so superstitious."

"Really?" he answered and put a glass behind the

bar. "Every driver except you has bought it in that car. That thing is cursed."

"Grey." It was Cecil. "We almost destroyed that vehicle."

"Hello, Cecil." He rarely took calls personally. "I'm glad you didn't. I need it."

"You know I'm not superstitious, but that car is sinister," Cecil said with a cough. "Are you certain I can't get something else for you?"

"No, thanks," I said. "Can you make sure the runes are at full strength?"

"Of course," he said. "You do realize every driver of that vehicle has met their demise within days of driving it?"

"Not everyone."

"Whatever it is you're up to out there, Grey, do try to be safe. I'll release it on the condition that once you're done with it, I decommission it—permanently."

"Agreed, once I'm done with it." The line clicked and switched back to Alice.

"Very well, Mr. Stryder," Alice said as she came back on. "Will you be keeping the Shroud, or shall we retrieve it?"

I glanced at Koda again. She was skilled with the bike. It was probably a good idea to keep a spare vehicle.

"I'll hold on to the Shroud for now."

"Excellent," I heard Koda say with a fist pump before she headed upstairs. "We need to change that name though."

"How long, Alice?" I shook my head.

"That vehicle was placed in protected storage at your

request," Alice said, tapping a keyboard. "We would need to fully retrofit and restore the runes—two hours should be sufficient. Will that be satisfactory?"

"Perfect, thank you, Alice," I said. "Please give my thanks to Cecil."

"I shall," she said and hung up.

I walked over to the bar. Frank was staring at me.

"Why didn't you fry them?" I handed Cole my glass. "Your idea of security is what—a strong dose of spit?"

"The Beast? Really?" Frank said, still staring. "You retired that thing because it was a death trap."

"If Lyrra is involved, I'm not going out on the Shroud." I motioned to Cole for a coffee. "The Beast is perfect, and you didn't answer my question."

"Your big ugly friend came over and released dampeners."

"He's not my friend." I took the hot mug from Cole. "How did he get past the door runes?"

"He didn't release the dampeners from *inside*," Frank said, giving me the 'are you really that dense' look. "He blasted the entire building with one of them, and then walked in like he owned the place."

"Shit, that's definitely a flaw in the defenses," I said.

"Oh, you think?" Frank said, clearly upset. "Especially when you're pissing off large angry Night Wardens and their twin fatal femmes."

"It's femme fatales."

"No, those two are just plain fatal," he spat, and Cole threw a runed towel over the small electrical blaze. "You sure you want to tangle with them again?"

"No, I'm not." I remembered the last time I'd faced that trio and shuddered at the thought. "Not much of a choice it seems, seeing as how Lyrra sent them to me."

"You'd better get some real security in here then, especially outside," Frank said with a glare. "You know, so we don't end up dead."

"Cole, tell Java I want the outside runed as well. I don't care about the cost," I said, savoring the coffee. "I want this place locked down in runes, inside and out. You"—I pointed at Frank—"upstairs."

He was in my room by the time I opened the door, parked on my ironwood trunk as he gave me his best dragon glare. I gave him a good hard stare in return and then sighed. I headed over to the worktable and pulled one of the empty vials to match the one filled with Redrum.

"Spit it out," I said and then added quickly, "I don't mean that literally."

"You plan on throwing her life away?"

The words gut-checked me.

"What the hell are you talking about?"

I knew exactly what he meant.

"I see how she looks at you," he said. "She lives for the excitement, the danger, the risk."

"She worked for Hades, she's used to living dangerously."

"Did *he* tell you what *she* did for him?" Frank asked. "For all you know, she could have been head broom pusher in one of his properties."

I actually didn't know what she did for him. I just assumed she was some kind of cleaner who had botched a job. That was one of the reasons I'd met with Corbel. I needed to know more about her.

"I don't know what she did for him...*yet*." I examined the empty vial and stepped over to the circle to make sure the defenses around the sword hadn't been compromised by Quinton's visit. "But I know she's trained, she took down a group of rummers, bypassed my security like it didn't exist, and saved my ass today."

"My original question stands."

"What do you want from me, Francis?" I said, raising my voice. "You want me to tell her to stay home? To stay out of my business? Do you think she'll listen?"

Frank shook his head as electricity sparked off him. "Not my place to tell you any of that, Grey," he said quietly. "I'm here to give you a heads up. You're using the Beast again and you're putting her in danger. Danger she may not be equipped to deal with. Jade's gone. I know you feel alone, but she can't take Jade's place."

"No one can," I said . "Thanks, Frank."

"I like the kid," he said and jumped off the trunk. "If she's going to stay, at the very least make sure she's Warden trained."

"I'll train her," I said, and Frank laughed. "What?"

"You just told me *she* saved *your* ass today," he said and started crackling. Electricity coruscated all over his body. "Your old ass can't train her. I'll get Yat."

"He's older than I am!"

"Yes, which means he's experienced," Frank said and spun in a circle. "You're just old and cranky."

"That may not be a good idea," I said. "She's Kano's granddaughter."

"The Fan?" Frank spat on the trunk again. "Does Yat know she's here?"

I grabbed a runed towel and put out the blaze. "What do you think?"

"He's the *only* one who can train her." He shook his head, sending small bolts of electricity everywhere. "Does she know anything?"

"Not enough to make a connection," I said. "Do you think it's the same Noh Fan? I'm pretty sure the name is popular."

"How many old stick and fan masters named Noh Fan Yat do *you* know?"

"One."

Frank nodded. "I'll speak with Yat," he said. "If she's using the fans, it's his obligation, even if she isn't related."

He disappeared a second later. I was going to have to listen to Master Yat expound on his favorite subject —the philosophy of pain.

I didn't envy Koda.

FIFTEEN

I STEPPED OVER to the circle where the sword floated lazily. Disabling the outer defenses and removing the book, I grabbed one of the elixirs from the worktable and matched the amount of liquid to the Redrum in the vial from Street.

I cast a minor mirroring defensive spell and pushed the shooting pain in my head to the back of my mind. The spell would trigger the moment someone tried to open the vial.

I held up both vials and made sure the liquids matched exactly in appearance. If they tested my copy, they would discover the mage equivalent to Viagra. I placed both vials in my duster and settled down to learn about the sword, when a knock interrupted me.

"What is it?" I yelled, not wanting to be bothered. "Is it too much to ask for twenty minutes of solitude?"

"I need to ask you something, Stryder," Koda said through the door. "This has been bugging me."

"Can't it wait?" I said. "How did you get past the hallway defenses anyway? Do you *want* to blow yourself apart?"

I could've sworn I'd reactivated the defenses when I set off the failsafe.

"What defenses?" she answered, and was about to knock again when I opened the door.

"How can I help you?" I cracked open the door, not moving from the entrance. "SuNaTran will deliver the Beast in about an hour. We'll go see Aria and get some answers. Why don't you go downstairs and eat something in the meantime? Cole makes a mean Reuben."

"How did Tessa know about my grandfather?"

"What do you mean?" I tried to stall. "Your grandfather was famous—one of the Hands of Fate. Those guys were insane."

"No one knows that story, Stryder," she said. "It's been wiped. At least that's what Hades told me. How does Tessa know? Was he lying?"

"No, not really." I opened the door and motioned for her to follow. She looked around in awe. "Come in."

"This place is huge—what the hell?"

"Time and relative distance in space design," I said. "Borrowed it from the Wordweavers, who borrowed it from a traveler from Galli—or was it Gorifreyan? All I know is that he was from some place in Ireland."

"Excuse me?" She was still looking around in shock. "You did what?"

"It's bigger on the inside than it is on the outside." I pointed to my duster that hung from the wall. "Like my pockets."

"Oh, why didn't you just say so?" She sat on the

ironwood trunk, which seemed to have become the unofficial sofa of my room. "How did she know?"

I put the sword book on the worktable and rubbed my face.

"The story of the Hand of Fate has been wiped from the collective consciousness," I said. "Only a few mages from each sect were allowed to retain the knowledge."

"What did they do?" she asked. "Why was it wiped?"

"I can't tell you." She crossed her arms and scowled. "No one can. That information was kept to the Elders of a few sects. All I know is that the five of them—three mages and a pair of brothers—went on a suicide mission. Most of them died and they helped stop the war."

"How did Tessa know about my grandfather?"

"She must have access to more information," I said. "Did you know?"

"Not when I was younger, no." She looked off to the side.

"Who told you?"

"The knowledge came with the fans."

"Excuse me?"

"When I was given the fans—it was like a floodgate of information." She looked back at me. "That was when I knew, but I didn't tell anyone."

It made sense. Certain runed weapons acted as repositories of information, holding specific techniques or methods of attack within the runes. Every new user operated with the accumulated knowledge of the previous owner.

It didn't work for just anyone though. The runed

weapon usually belonged to a specific bloodline. In this case Kano's.

"Did your father use the fans?"

She shook her head. "He hated them." She flicked her wrist, materializing a fan in her hand. "He blamed them for taking away my grandfather."

"How did you get them?"

"My great-uncle made sure I got them when I was old enough," she said. "He promised to train me when I was ready."

"This great-uncle have a name?" I asked, trying to gauge how much she knew. "Is he still alive?"

"I don't know, he disappeared right after he gave me the fans. That was years ago." She shrugged, but I could tell it bothered her. "I tried looking for him, but nothing. Now I wouldn't know where to start."

"What was his name?" I asked again. "Maybe I can ask around."

"He went by Noh Fan, but I don't know if that was his real name," she said, putting away the fan. "At this point, I don't even remember what he looks like. It was so long ago."

I turned away to hide my surprise. She was due for a family reunion sooner than she thought. Master Yat's full name was Noh Fan Yat. It was entirely possible he was part of the Hand of Fate—one of the two who survived the suicide mission. He had never shared, and I had never asked.

"I'll ask around." I kept my voice even. "Maybe he's still around."

"I doubt it," she said. "Wouldn't family try and find each other?"

"Sometimes there are situations we can't control."

"Can I ask you something, Stryder?"

"Sure." I picked up the sword book from the table. "As long as it doesn't have to do with—shit."

I held up the book and the runes glowed in response. They were moving around randomly, something I hadn't noticed the last time I held it.

"What's that—your diary?" she asked.

I debated telling her the truth for a few seconds.

I pointed at the sword. "It came with that. Tells me the history of the blade."

"Is that the blade Hades gave you?" She narrowed her eyes and shook her head. "It feels wrong somehow. Like it's there, but not really there."

"Make sure you don't touch it and I mean ever," I said, knowing how easily she circumvented runic defenses. "I'm serious. This isn't like the Shroud. You touch that thing and it's over." I didn't really know what would happen, but I figured a little fear would be good.

She shuddered in response. "It feels alive."

I nodded. "Supposed to be able to help me with my condition."

"Is it that powerful?" she said, leaning forward to take a closer look. "Enough to reverse an entropic dissolution?"

"Reverse it? No, nothing can do that." I shook my head. "It's supposed to stop what's happening." I nudged her back a few feet. "Every time I grab it, it jumps in my hand like it's happy to see me. It creeps me the hell out."

"Maybe it's alive, and it's trying to jump *out* of your hand, not *into*."

"Was that your attempt at humor?" I asked. "Stick to the fans."

She gave me a scowl before continuing. I quickly realized that my days of quiet solitude had abruptly ended.

"Are you going to use it?" She approached the circle again but wisely stayed near the outer edge of the perimeter.

"What?" I murmured, feeling distracted. The runes on the book had shifted location and order—the equivalent of a combination lock. That usually meant an enormous amount of power had gone into creating the defensive spell. If I tried to open the book the wrong way, the results would be nasty.

"The sword Hades gave you. You plan on using it?"

"You may not have noticed, but I'm not getting along with magic much these days."

"But you're dying." She stared at me. "And it can help you."

"So what?" I snapped back, irritated. "We're *all* dying. I'm not going to use some weapon that needs me as a host. I have Fatebringer" —I tapped my holster—"that's enough."

"Until it isn't," Koda muttered under her breath.

"What *do* you want?" I asked, frustrated. I had grown unaccustomed to having people in my space. "Why are *you* here?"

"I want out," she said, stepping closer to me. "And for that to happen, you need to be alive."

"Out of what?"

"Everything." She headed for the door. "All of it, Hades, the targets, the killing—everything."

"You *were* an assassin," I said more to myself than to her. "I've never heard of him letting one of his assassins leave his service alive—except Corbel, who declined."

"I was Corbel's second." She stopped at the door and spoke without turning. "The only one to survive the training out of my group."

It explained Hades' actions. If he retired her, it would give the appearance of poor judgment on his part. Which, in his world, probably meant weakness. If he didn't exile her, it would seem like favoritism. She would become a target and used against him. Again, weakness.

By placing her with me, a disgraced ex-Night Warden, he diminished her status enough to make her invisible without removing her entirely. I was the perfect solution.

"Shit," I muttered, grasping the enormity of the play. "Did you know?"

She turned and glared at me for a second before shaking her head. "Do you really think Hades consults with *anyone* before setting his plans in motion?" she said, her voice grim. "Whatever is killing you must be starting with the few brain cells you have left. I'll be downstairs."

I wasn't going to wait two days for my answers. I pulled out my phone and was about to follow her downstairs when the sword spoke.

SIXTEEN

AT FIRST, I was sure it was Frank.

"Mage," said a voice from the direction of the sword that floated lazily in the center of the runic circle. "We must speak."

"Nice one, Francis." I dropped the book on the worktable. "Cut the crap. It's not funny."

"There is nothing humorous about your situation, mage," the voice said. "You are dying."

Frank would never speak that way. There was no trace of chlorine in the air, and his usual tone was absent. The only explanation had to be that I was losing my mind. The voice was distinctly feminine, and I realized 'her' voice wasn't audible.

"Damn, now I'm hearing voices. This dying thing is going to truly suck if I'm out of my mind while I do it."

"You are not hearing voices. You are hearing one voice—mine."

"And to whom might I be speaking?" I looked under the worktable and in the corner near the sword. "I swear, Frank, if I find out this is you, I *will* crush you, lizard."

"Focus, Mage." An orb of black energy formed in the circle holding the sword. The orb bobbed in the circle for a few seconds before racing at me. I put up an arm, wishing I had kept my duster on as it slammed into my chest and tossed me across the floor. I landed in a heap, staring at the ceiling. "Do I have your attention now?"

"You do and the answer is: no." I lay motionless and did a mental inventory, making sure only my pride was bruised. "Whatever it is you want, the answer is no."

"You fear me?" the sword said.

I got up slowly and made my way back to the circle. Everything ached, but I was certain it could've hit me with something worse. Several of the muscles in my arms spasmed as I approached—a telltale sign of a nerve inhibitor spell. Even if I could cast, my forearms were flexed, locking my hands into claws. Casting would have been impossible.

I shook out my hands as I took a deep breath. I didn't know what I was dealing with exactly, so it was best to measure my response.

"How did you manage to cast from *inside* a null circle?" I stayed a good five feet away from the sword. The effects of the inhibitor spell began to wear off. I flexed my fingers.

"This cage cannot contain me," it said as it floated out of the circle. "I was merely humoring you."

"Shit," I said, backing up and getting ready to cast. "Can you stay over there?"

"You *do* fear me." It remained in place as it floated

by the worktable. "Perhaps you do possess some wisdom."

"I don't *fear* you—I just prefer to keep some distance between us. That's all."

"You lie poorly." It floated back into the circle, and I let out the breath I didn't know I was holding. "We must bond."

"No, thank you," I said. "I don't do talking swords or swords at all, for that matter. Not when I have Fatebringer."

I adjusted my holster and patted the butt of my gun.

"Your weapon is inadequate," she said. "It does not contain enough power to defeat the one who held me —I do."

"It doesn't speak either. Silence is a trait I prefer in my weapons." I looked up suddenly at her last words. "Excuse me? You *do* what?"

"Your weapon cannot defeat the one you call Hades."

"And you can?" I said, incredulous. "He's an old god. One of the oldest."

"He *is* old, I am older."

"Who are you?" I backed up even farther.

"You may address me as Izanami," she said. "While this Hades is formidable—together we can face him."

"As your host?"

"You are dying, Mage," she said. "Do you wish to end your existence? I can undo the spell that lies within your body."

I gestured and black runes flowed over the circle. Blinding pain shot up one side of my face as the mother of all migraines squeezed my skull in a vise-like grip. Black tendrils of energy shot out of the circle and impaled the sword in place.

"That's more of a reason to keep away from you." I held my head. "And to keep you away from everyone." I gestured one final time, ratcheting the pain into the stratosphere.

"Your cage is impressive, but ultimately futile," she said. "It will only hold me for a short time."

"Long enough for me to do my homework." I grabbed the sword book from the worktable and backed out of my room. I activated the runes on my doorframe to ensure no one would enter. "Should've left the damn sword alone."

SEVENTEEN

I STUMBLED DOWNSTAIRS as the drumline in my head began a skull-shattering cadence of obliteration.

"Cole!" I yelled from the stairs. "Deathwish!"

Caffeine was the only thing that calmed the ice pick in my skull. Deathwish coffee curbed the migraine effects of casting. By the time I got downstairs, a steaming mug of black coffee resembling ink sat on the bar.

The concern on Koda's face let me know I looked how I felt. "What happened to you? That smells like it should come with a warning label. Are you planning on drinking—?"

I raised a hand in response, grabbed the mug, and took a long sip of steaming javambrosia. The reaction was almost immediate. The drumline was reduced to one congo player and I could think straight again. I pulled out my phone and pressed the speed dial for Corbel.

"What?" he said when he answered. "I told you two days."

"No, tonight." I clenched against the pain that threatened to rise again and downed the rest of my coffee. "You need to come get your boss's psycho sword and answer my questions."

"Where?" he said with a sigh. "Don't say The Dive. You have a few of your friends watching you and I would prefer not to erase any Night Wardens tonight."

I'd expected Lyrra to keep my place under surveillance. It's what I would do. If they saw Corbel, it was possible they would attack—if they were feeling suicidal.

"My ride will be here within the hour," I said. "Patience and Fortitude, two hours."

"Don't be late. And don't bring your friends."

He ended the call, and I handed Cole my empty mug. The pain in my head subsided to a dull throb.

"Where's General Java?" I looked at Cole. "I need these runes done tonight."

"Said he's on his way," Cole answered as he removed five-pound bags of coffee from under the bar. "How many do you want to give him?"

"As many as he wants." I was about to dial SuNaTran, when I heard the truck backing up. "It's here."

"You should just destroy that thing." Cole shuddered and shook his head. "That car is evil."

"A car is an inanimate object." I headed to the door. "How is a car evil?" As soon as the words left my lips, I thought about the sword in my room.

"Oh, you're saying it's misunderstood?"

"No, I'm saying there's a difference between cursed and evil." I opened the door and saw Robert backing up a flatbed truck with the Beast on the back. "The Beast is cursed—not evil."

"Wait, what?" Koda asked, heading to the door. "You requested a *cursed* vehicle?"

The flatbed stopped moving. The rear of the truck began inclining upward. When it was at the proper angle, Robert moved a lever, releasing it onto the sidewalk in front of The Dive. Robert moved the truck and stepped out. Normally SuNaTran drove the vehicles to their locations—this wasn't a normal situation.

"Good evening, sir." He held out a clipboard. "Are you certain about this?"

I grabbed the clipboard and nodded. "Completely." I placed a thumb on the biometric area reserved for signing. "Please give Cecil my regards."

"Will do." He tipped his cap, jumped back into the truck, and pulled away.

Sitting there like some otherworldly creature was the Beast. Based on a 1970 Chevy Camaro, SuNaTran had made some modifications. Like the Phantoms they provided, the Beast was equipped with armor plating where it mattered. After Jade, it felt wrong to drive it, but if Lyrra was going to hunt me on the streets, there was no better vehicle to be in.

"That's one sweet ride," Koda said with a whistle. "Is it really cursed?"

"Just ask the three previous drivers—oh, wait, you can't because they're all dead," Cole said from behind us as he stood in the doorway. "Whatever you do, Koda, leave the driving to him. I'm serious."

"He's right." I placed my hand on the driver's side

door, and a wave of orange energy danced across its surface, unlocking it. I sat behind the wheel and turned on the engine. The rumble was low and throaty, just like I remembered. "I seem to be immune to the curse because of my condition."

"I think that evil thing just likes him." Cole stepped away. "Its soul is as black as the driver's."

I could see the black smoke wafting up from its surface. I placed my hands on the wheel, and red runes came to life along the dashboard. They pulsed for thirty seconds, and then disappeared.

"What was that?" Koda asked as she looked into the car.

"It was reading my runic signature—meaning no one else can drive the Beast."

"Runic biometrics." Koda raised an eyebrow. "That's beyond cutting-edge."

"I'm just glad it's still black and not purple." I walked back into The Dive. "The last thing I want to be driving is the Grape."

"What?" Koda asked as I headed upstairs and then stopped.

"Long story—for some reason Cecil likes byzantium, and some of his tech mages imbue the color with defensive properties, which he then applies to working vehicles."

"But he didn't paint the Beast?"

"He tried," I said with a small smile. "The paint burned right off and left the matte black you see now. The Beast doesn't like to be purple."

"Like I said, black car with a black soul—just like the driver," Cole said as he pulled out more coffee bags.

"You plan on giving Java our entire stock?"

"This isn't Deathwish—he only drinks Odinforce blend." Cole stacked a few more bags on the bar. "Your inventory is safe, don't worry."

"It'd better be." I turned to Koda. "I need to go see the Hound and return the demon sword his boss tried to enslave me with."

"Corbel?" she asked. "Will Hades be there?"

"I'm not expecting him, but you never know with gods."

"I'm coming with you," she said, crossing her arms. "Just in case he does show up."

"I'm sure your presence will intimidate him."

She glared at me and set her jaw. There was no way I was going to leave her at The Dive. Her uncanny ability to bypass runes concerned me. My room held a few artifacts that could level the entire block if mishandled. I wasn't in the mood to come home to a crater because of her curiosity.

She pointed at me. "I'm not letting you face him or Corbel alone. I don't trust them."

"Smartest thing you've said all day." I turned to head upstairs. "I'll be down in a few."

"Stryder," she said, "you need to be careful with them. Hades never shows his real hand. There's always a plan behind a plan with him. When you think you've figured him out, he's twenty moves ahead."

"Not this time," I said as I climbed the steps. "This time I'm not playing his game. He gets his sword back and we walk away."

"It's never that easy." She headed downstairs to the bar.

I took a deep breath and braced myself. An ancient spirit trapped in a sword that wanted me as its host. What could possibly go wrong?

EIGHTEEN

I OPENED THE door and the sensation of biting into a large lemon, peel and all, flooded my senses, nearly making me choke.

It never failed with strong ambient magic, and my room was thick with it. The black runes I had placed around the sword were gone. It floated freely in the center of the containment circle. White runes floated lazily around the perimeter. They shone with an intensity that made it difficult to stare at them directly.

"Mage, you've come to your senses at last."

I nodded and narrowed my eyes, trying to decipher the runes around the circle. I'd never seen runes filled with such energy. This was going to be trickier than I thought.

Why hadn't it left the circle? Then I saw it. The white runes were mirror images of the ones I'd placed around the circle. It was trying to invert my containment runes. A simple and elegant solution that would never work.

"Nice try on the inversion casting." I placed my

hand on the ironwood trunk. Several runes arranged themselves in sequence, and the lock clicked open. "Won't work, though."

I carefully sifted through the contents, looking for a particular artifact.

"Release me, mage," Izanami said after a few moments. "You know we must bond."

"One sec," I said, still looking through the trunk. I found what I was looking for and stood. I held a small piece of fabric and approached the circle, careful not to breach the perimeter. "I need to move you, and there's no way I am grabbing you without protection."

"Protection? You do not need protection from me, mage."

I tossed the piece of fabric into the circle and it flashed as it hit the sword, nearly blinding me.

"That,"—I pointed to the lattice of orange energy forming around the sword—"is a Lazarus lattice. Anything magical touched by it is rendered inert."

"You will not contain me with such primitive magic."

"Not by itself, no," I answered, touching the edge of the circle. "But the runes you tried to invert weren't only containment runes. You couldn't invert them because they're siphons—slowly draining you until I could use the lattice."

"You weaved the siphon into the containment—that was clever."

"Yes. That way, the more you tried to escape, the more energy fed the spell." I narrowed my eyes and saw the lattice surround the sword. "Subtle but effective."

The fact that I could still hear her made me

conscious of how much power the sword held. A mage hit with a Lazarus lattice lost all magical ability upon contact. That she could still communicate, even after it had enveloped the sword, meant it contained off-the-charts power. I couldn't see Hades giving me this thing as a gesture of goodwill.

"I have read your runic signature," Izanami said as I reached out and grabbed the sword. It didn't jump this time. "Touch my blade, allow me to sate my thirst with your life's blood, and we shall be one. I can heal you."

"Do you hear how twisted you just sounded?" I said, looking at the sword. "I'm taking you back to Hades. I don't want you. More importantly I don't *need* you."

"That would be a mistake."

"The mistake would be bonding to some blood-drinking sword," I snapped back. "Was that supposed to be your invitation?"

"Yes. Did you not find it appealing?"

I shook my head. "Can anyone else hear you?"

"Only my host can hear me."

"We aren't bonded."

"Not fully, no," she said. "All that remains is more of your life-blood. Each time you held me, I siphoned some of your life force, which caused my sudden motion. You might even say it was…subtle but effective."

"Wait, Corbel and Hades both held you," I said, quickly. "Why aren't you bonded to either of them?"

"Hades is a god, so to bond with an entity on that level would mutually negate our existence," she replied. "I was created to destroy the supernatural—not empower it."

"What about Corbel?" I rubbed my face in frustration. This was getting worse by the second. "He isn't a god."

"But he *is* bonded to one. *You* are my ideal host."

"This can't be happening." I placed a hand on the trunk, locking it. "I'm still giving you back."

"That action will accelerate your deteriorating condition."

"Hades knew this would happen—didn't he?"

"I am not imbued with telepathic abilities. I cannot say if he knew or not."

"Are you saying if I give you back I'll just die faster?" I held the sword out and glared at it. "Just from touching you twice?"

"See for yourself, mage," she said. "Use your sight."

I narrowed my eyes and examined the sword. At first I didn't see anything and was about to stop, when I saw them hundreds of filaments no thicker than a hair connected us.

"What the hell are those?"

"Runic conduits," she whispered. "Do you understand now why we must bond? To sever them is to sever your existence."

I had never seen runic conduits, but Ziller mentioned it in his treatise on magical symbiosis. His work didn't relate to some spirit-filled sword, but the principle was the same. Runic conduits formed between entities sharing a life-force for a prolonged period of time. The problem here was that I only touched the sword twice, and conduits were supposed to form over years.

"How?"

"I'm much older than you can imagine and have forgotten things you are still yet to learn," she answered. "Can you grasp your situation now?"

I put the sword down on the trunk and put on my duster.

"I do, and all I can say is fuck you, *and* Hades."

"Your anger does not change your situation," she said. "We must still bo—"

I shoved the sword in the secret pocket, shutting her up. Hades had played me like a rookie. Corbel was right —he read me and pushed all the right buttons. I felt the rage and frustration rise. Black energy leaked out of my hands and set my head on fire as the pain rushed in. I unleashed a blast of dark magic and fell to my knees, gasping as footsteps rushed up the stairs. I sensed Cole at the doorway. Behind him stood Koda.

"Grey?" he called out. He knew not to enter. The runes around the door pulsed a bright orange, indicating they were active. "You can't keep doing this."

I raised an arm to indicate I was good. I wasn't, but Cole could be worse than Roxanne when it came to my condition. I looked up to see Koda step into the room without being blasted to bits.

"How the hell did you do that?" Cole stepped back, shaking his head.

"I'll deal with it," I rasped and put a hand on the trunk to steady myself. "Can I get some—?"

"Deathwish, I'm on it." Cole headed downstairs. "I'll make it to go."

I nodded silent thanks. Koda snaked an arm under mine and helped me sit on the trunk. I looked at her for a long while before speaking.

"You're not supposed to be able to do that."

"What, lift your old ass from the floor?"

I pointed to the door. The runes still pulsed their bright orange. "If Cole had tried to walk through that door, we'd be picking up pieces of him right now."

She turned to the door and gave me a short nod, her face grim. "Like I've been saying—your security sucks."

"No." I shook my head. "I know for a fact you should be ghosted because *I* placed those runes, not Java."

"What the hell happened in here?" she said, trying to deflect. "Downstairs lit up like Times Square and Cole nearly lost it."

"How?" I got to my feet. "Tell me, or I can arrange to drop you off together with the psycho sword."

She looked up suddenly. Fear flitted across her face for a split second, followed immediately by anger. I felt like shit for using the threat, but I didn't trust anyone. Especially not someone who could stroll through my defenses as if they didn't exist.

"In order to use the fans in my family you have to be a genetic outlier," she said with a sigh. "I think that's the real reason my father never used them. I think he wanted to, but my grandfather instructed my grand-uncle not to pass the fans to him."

"What are you?" I asked as my head began to clear. "I mean I know you're human, but how do you walk through my door and not explode, or start the Shroud, and disassemble Fatebringer?"

"I'm what's known as a runic cipher."

"Impossible," I scoffed. "That's a myth. Everyone has some kind of energy signature—everyone."

She cocked her head to one side, placed her hands on her hips, and smiled. "Are you always this dense? Or were you dropped on your head repeatedly as a child?"

"It's a gift." I moved to the worktable. I grabbed the sword book and placed it in the center of the containment circle. I crouched down to activate the runes, and the circle thrummed with energy. I pointed at the book. "Show me."

She walked over to the circle, crouched down, and remained motionless for a few seconds. She narrowed her eyes, snatched the book from the center, and tossed it to me.

"I can see why Hades wanted you to work for him." I held the book up and then looked at her. "The circle didn't even 'see' you. It's not my security—you're a freak."

Her expression darkened. "Among other things, yes."

"Hey, I didn't mean it like that," I fumbled. "It's just ciphers are supposed to be impossible."

"I've been called worse." She stood and headed to the door. "I'll meet you downstairs."

There was no way Hades would retire her. She could bypass any runic defense and emerge unscathed. No one and nothing was safe from her.

I rolled up a piece of paper, tossed it at the circle, and watched it fall to the ground in a pile of ash. I looked at the sword book in my hand. There wasn't a trace of damage—not even a singed page. Whatever ability she possessed was transferable by touch. This was a dangerous ability.

I locked the door and headed downstairs. This situation was getting better by the hour.

NINETEEN

WE ARRIVED AT The New York Public Library with plenty of time to spare. Several locations in the city were designated places of power. The library was rumored to contain an underground vault that possessed magical artifacts. No one had ever discovered this vault, but it was undeniable that ambient magic permeated the area. The sensation of biting into a candy apple, sweet followed by sour, hit me as I parked the Beast in front of the famous stone lions, Patience and Fortitude. Corbel stood next to the northernmost one, Fortitude.

"I need you to stay here." I handed her a subdermal communicator. "You switch it on here" —I indicated where she needed to press—"and you'll be able to hear the conversation. Turns off the same way."

"Are you seriously telling me to stay in the car?"

"For now, yes." I looked around us. "I don't trust him any more than you do. I don't know if he came alone; and if he didn't, I would rather not give away that you're here."

"He could just sense me, you know—'hound of Hades' and all that?"

"Not in here." I flipped a switch and the windshield polarized. All the other windows were tinted to restrict anyone from seeing inside. "The runes on the Beast won't let him."

I didn't go into how the curse acted like a constant jamming signal, causing active pain to anyone trying to scan the Beast. I strode up to Corbel and the lions, admiring them as I always did. It always felt like they were about to leap off their pedestals into the street and tear traffic to shreds.

"I can't believe SuNaTran released that menace to you—again."

"What can I say, Cecil likes me," I said with a short nod. "He did promise to destroy it this time."

"I don't know why he bothers, it didn't take the last time. That vehicle is indestructible," Corbel said, shaking his head. "The fallout from that incident prompted a visit from Hades."

"Could be he has something more powerful this time." I shrugged. "A nuclear option like a super entropic spell. Maybe he'll get Mr. Tea and Crumpets to unleash another void vortex and I can drive it in?"

Corbel just stared at me. "Both of you are insane. Inform me when he's about to start the process so I can leave the city for a while."

"Done," I said, looking at his pained expression. "You want to go for a walk?"

He nodded. "Let's just put some distance between us and your deathmobile." He rubbed his temples. "Thing always gave me a headache."

I climbed the steps, and he kept pace beside me.

"Did anyone follow you?" he asked, looking around.

"You tell me."

He closed his eyes and nodded. "Seems like you left your Night Warden babysitters at home."

"No one follows the Beast for long," I said. "Where's your escort?"

"They have the block cordoned off, with a subtle 'stay away' casting that should ensure us some privacy."

The same way Hades rarely traveled without his Hound, Corbel rarely traveled without a tribus-bellum —three mages I called the Shades. A traditional tribus contained offense, defense, and healing. The Shades were just different levels of destruction—wholesale, total, and massive. The last time I faced off against them, I was still able to cast and barely escaped with my life. I didn't want to face them now.

"I'm flattered."

"It sounded urgent, considering I told you two days, and here we are."

We walked around the building and onto the lawn of Bryant Park. The sweet/sour taste was stronger here. I heard the delicate melody of the active spell around us.

"Why didn't you tell me she was a cipher?"

"Would it have made a difference?"

I was conscious of the subdermal in my ear.

"No, I still would've agreed." I reached into my pocket and removed the sword. "*This,* on the other hand, needs to go back to your boss."

"You're going to have to show me how you do that one day." Looking at me as I pulled out the sword from my duster. Narrowing his eyes at me and then the sword, he sighed. "I can't."

"What do you mean you can't?" I said, raising my voice. "This *thing*" —I shook the sword at him —"wants me as its host. The last thing it said was I needed to let it sate itself on my life-blood."

"You should."

"Are you insane? I'm not going to let some bloodthirsty sword drink its fill of me."

"What's the alternative?"

"I return it. He said—"

"No, you're two-thirds of the way in on this now," he said with a shake of his head. "Hades takes that sword back and let me share what will happen: you die."

"Tell me something I don't know."

"Almost immediately."

"Okay, *that* I didn't know. Shit."

"That sword was created to destroy beings like Hades and his kind." He gave me a hard look. "If he takes it back, which he can't, there would be an inevitable reaction and outcome—think matter and anti-matter."

"He knew. The bastard," I said, realizing now I couldn't return the sword. "He knew I wouldn't risk it."

Frank's words came back to me. *He knows you. Better than you know yourself.*

"Stryder," he started with a sigh, "I don't like you, but I do respect you. I consider you a necessary evil in our city. One that must exist to stop some of the nastier things that roam the streets."

"Anyone ever tell you that you have a way with words?"

"Listen to what I'm saying—for once." He stopped and sniffed the air. "We have guests incoming."

"Guests?" I asked, looking around.

"I can't stay, so listen." He grabbed my arm. "If you bond to the sword, you become a real threat to Hades and any being on his power level."

"I also become a target, so thanks, but no thanks." I shrugged off his arm. "You have anything else to share about Koda?"

"She's talented, gifted, and deadly," he said. "Try not to piss her off and you should get along.

"I know all that, I meant about her being a cipher."

"That drove Hades crazy too," he said with a chuckle and then grew serious. "You're going to have to trust her, Stryder, or get better locks."

"She bypasses everything in my place."

"A piece of advice," he said. "Ciphers are considered nil, nothing, both figuratively and literally. In a different age, when no energy signature could be found, they were killed at birth."

"I didn't even think they could exist before today."

"Try a little kindness; treat her like a person and you won't have to invest in stronger runic defenses."

"I don't do *trust*, Corbel."

"I don't see you have much of a choice. I'll keep in touch."

He stepped back, faded out, and disappeared. The delicate melody was replaced with the foghorn of destruction. The sweet/sour of the library was followed by an aftertaste of old coffee.

"Guests, my ass," I muttered as I ran back to the Beast and stopped short at the edge of the park.

"Koda, we have incoming. Prepare for—"

"Oh, are you talking to me?" she responded. "Are you sure I can help you? It's hard to know who to trust these days."

"Cut the crap," I growled. "If you're this bent, we can talk it out later. Right now we have rummers to deal with." She dropped her camouflage and appeared next to me. Her masking had kept her hidden from my senses. I gave her a nod and grunted begrudgingly. "Not bad."

"You'd better believe we're talking this out later, in a language you understand—on the second floor." She materialized her fans and stepped away from me. "Are you using that?" She pointed to the sword in my hand.

I shook myself out of my shock, put the sword in a pocket, and drew Fatebringer. A pack of rummers, followed by several ogres, was coming our way.

TWENTY

THEY STREAMED IN from the north side of the park. This placed them between the Beast and us. I counted over twenty rummers and three ogres. This was getting out of hand. The rummers I understood, but the ogres made no sense.

"We cut a path through them and get to the Beast," I said as they approached. "Then we bug out, clear?"

She nodded, and I made sure Fatebringer was loaded with negation rounds. "Let's do this." I saw her eyes flash red. "I'll take the rummers."

"I'll go have a chat with the ogres."

She nodded and raced off. I didn't have much time to focus on her before the first ogre closed on me.

"Time to die, wizard," it said with a grunt and swung. Ogres relied on their brute strength and near invulnerability to magic when they fought.

Unfortunately for them, I didn't use magic. I ducked under the swing and fired Fatebringer three times point-blank. The negation rounds punched into the ogre, staggering it. A few seconds later, the rounds reduced the ogre to dust.

"Oh, these will be banned soon, I'm sure," I muttered, looking at the pile of ogre dust as a kick from behind launched me across the field. Ogre number two caught me unawares, and would have shattered my spine if it weren't for my duster absorbing and dissipating the blow over its surface. The only downside was the increased heat.

I gave Aria silent thanks as I rolled on the grass and came up firing. I fired twice, two shots center mass. Ogre number two burst into dust. I grabbed a speed loader and reloaded Fatebringer as a fist rushed at my head. How were they moving so fast? I managed to turn and duck and didn't see the other fist rush into my side. Again, the duster saved me from multiple broken parts as I sailed across and bounced over the lawn.

I felt the ogre closing in—fast. Sweat poured down my face as I tried to get a bead on the incoming agent of massive pain. My hand shook as I fired twice, hitting the ogre with no effect. I took a two-handed grip on Fatebringer and fired again—the rounds about as effective as pillows. I holstered my gun, cursed, and reached into the pocket, pulling out the sword.

Black tendrils burst forth in every direction as the ogre bore down. I stood shakily and felt a surge of power as the tendrils slammed into my body.

"Come, beast," I heard myself say. "Race to your doom."

I stepped forward as the ogre rushed at me. At the last second, I twisted and executed a single-handed rising diagonal cut to the upper right, going into a descending diagonal cut to the lower left.

The ogre took one more step forward before falling to the ground and dissolving. Energy flooded my body, and I raced to the rummers surrounding Koda. I stopped some distance away and struggled to sheathe the sword.

"Don't be foolish, mage," Izanami said as she pushed against me, resisting. "Together we can dispatch these foul creatures."

"I got this, thanks," I said through clenched teeth, managing to sheathe the sword and put it back in the pocket. I drew Fatebringer and fired several times, dropping rummers with each shot. "Time to go!"

Koda slashed her way through several rummers as we ran for the Beast. "Where are the ogres?" she asked as we ran.

"Retired," I said as we rounded the corner of the library and bounded down the steps with the rummers close behind. She got in, and I slid across the hood to jump in the driver's side. I saw rummers falling down the steps as I started the engine and pulled away.

I raced uptown as my heart beat a machine-gun rhythm in my chest.

"I've never seen ogres move that fast." She sighed as she rested her head back in the seat. "How did you manage all three?"

"Negation rounds—for the win." I clenched the steering wheel with a white-knuckle grip as the power flowed inside me, and I stepped on the gas.

"Stryder?" Koda's voice was distant noise as I stepped down harder on the gas pedal. "Stryder!"

She grabbed hold of the wheel and pulled. I felt her tug against me as we avoided the truck that had stopped ahead of us. I stepped on the brakes and we screeched to a halt. I jumped out of the car, the power flowing through me and looking for an outlet. I let it bleed out of me and formed two orbs of black energy.

"Get back in the car," I said, my voice hoarse with pain. "I can't hold on to this."

"What is it?" she said, staying on the far side of the Beast. "What happened to you?"

The howl ripped through my chest as I fell to my knees, releasing the orbs in a wave of pent up energy. The sword materialized in my hand. I swung the blade around me, bleeding off more dark energy. For a few seconds, I felt whole again. Magic coursed through my body, vibrant and alive, a part of me. Then it was gone, along with the sword. Replaced by a void I couldn't fill.

"Haven—Roxanne," I managed, before falling face-first into the street and blacking out.

TWENTY-ONE

BRIGHT LIGHTS BLINDED me as I tried to keep my eyes closed against them. I lay in a large restrictive bed. Rancid old coffee flooded my sense of taste—Haven. I saw the bandages on my arms and chest. The rummers must have had a field day.

"I could really use a gallon of Deathwish right now," I muttered without opening my eyes. "What time is it?"

"You really are quite stubborn."

I recognized the voice and accent—Mr. Tea and Crumpets. I opened my eyes then and took in the scene.

Roxanne stood to one side of my bed checking my vitals. She held a clipboard and looked like she wanted to crack me upside the head with it. A little further back sat Koda, who stared at me with concern. On the other side sat Mr. Tea and Crumpets.

I looked up at Roxanne accusingly and scowled.

"Don't you dare give me that look." She checked the IV in my arm. "You nearly killed yourself tonight."

"I'm fine." I tried to sit up and failed. "What did you

give me?"

"Something to keep you off your feet for a while." She pointed at my chest. "You'll leave when *I* think you're ready to leave. Not one second sooner. You fight me on this, and I can guarantee you a world of pain. Do you understand, Grey?"

"I understand that you're making a big deal out of nothing." I glanced over at the mage. "And I told you *not* to call him."

Roxanne stepped close to the bed and got in my face. The anger came off her in waves. I'd only ever seen her this angry a few times in my life. A troll had managed to get into Haven once and was headed for pediatrics. Roxanne took it down and nearly destroyed the floor in the process. There wasn't much left of the troll when she was done.

"And I told you *not* to cast." She narrowed her eyes at me. "And don't tell me you didn't cast. There's a crater in the middle of 6th Avenue they're calling a water main break, thanks to you not casting."

"Excuse me?"

I had no recollection of what she was talking about. It must have showed on my face because she stepped back and gestured to the mage.

"This is what I have to deal with." She waved a hand at me. "He doesn't even remember what happened."

"No, no…" I raised a hand in protest. "I remember."

"Tell me how you got here, Grey." She placed the clipboard slowly on the side table. "Did you walk, teleport, fly, or did Koda have to drive you in your infernal car to bring you here?"

I drew a complete blank, but it had to be bad if Koda drove the Beast. I remembered the sword filling me with power, most of it dark, and then falling. I must have said Haven or something close for Koda to bring me here.

"I'm going to go with Koda driving the Beast for four-hundred, Alex."

"I know you think this is a game," she said softly, which actually concerned me. "This is bad enough when it's your life on the line, but now it's not just your life, is it?"

"Rox, I'm—"

"Koda," she said, ignoring me. "Come with me. I need to run some tests to make sure there are no residual side-effects from Mr. Stryder's reckless use of dark magic."

"Come on, Rox, you're overreacting." I pushed up on the bed. "I'm okay. Nothing happened."

Koda fell in behind her as Roxanne stopped at the door and turned to the mage.

"Tristan, talk some sense into him before I keep him in an extended medically-induced coma." She glared at me and cut off any response I had. "I think one hundred years would be a good nap. What do you think, Grey?"

They left the room and Tristan Montague stared at me.

TWENTY-TWO

"HELLO, GREY." HE steepled his fingers as he looked at me. "Where is it?"

I narrowed my eyes at him and saw he had shifted recently. I was older, by about a century, but he could cast. I'd say things were about even if it came to a confrontation. Last time I fought a battle mage, we leveled a city block. In my defense, the battle mage started it—I just finished it.

"Blow up any buildings lately?" I pointed to my duster. "It's over there, inside pocket."

He gave a short nod, ignored my comment, and brought my coat to the bed. He was doing the serious, conscientious magic-user routine, and it was aggravating me. He was dressed in his usual suit. What was it with some mages and suits? His hair was all over the place and he looked like a Einstein on a bad hair day.

"Have you ever heard of hair gel?" I motioned around my head. "You don't even need magic for it to work."

"When I sent that sword to Hades, I didn't expect him to give it to a dark mage." He reached into the pocket and pulled out the sword. "I certainly didn't expect that dark mage to be you."

"*You* sent him that sword?" I couldn't hide my surprise. "Where did you get it?"

"It's complicated." He narrowed his eyes as he held the sword and shook his head. "Bloody hell, you're practically bonded to it."

I nodded. "She likes me." I crossed my hands behind my head. "We may even move in together."

He drew the black blade, and the red runes along its length pulsed with power. "If this is anything like Simon's Ebonsoul, all it needs now is—"

"Blood," I finished. "It keeps reminding me."

"It communicates with you?"

"*She* does, yes."

"She?"

"Female voice. Goes by the name of Izanami."

"Izanami?" he said and rubbed his chin—that always annoyed the hell out of me. "The goddess of creation and death?"

"Is there another Izanami?"

"Do you understand the ramifications of this?" He ignored my gibe, using his best professor-lecture-hall voice. "What were you thinking?"

"Are you trying to tell me this is a bad idea?" I answered. "Because we've raced past bad idea and entered into full-blown nightmare."

"Grey, you unleashed an entropic wave in the middle of the city." He placed the sword down on the bed. "The only thing that saved your partner was that she had the presence of mind to enclose herself in your vehicle."

"Shit, how bad is it?"

"You heard Roxanne—6th Avenue is a war zone, complete with a huge crater in the center of 42nd Street. What the bloody hell happened?"

"I don't know." I shifted in the bed. "Most of it is hazy. I cut down some ogres, fast ones, and it siphoned power into me—a lot of power."

"More than you could handle," he said quietly.

He narrowed his eyes at me and I sensed the quiet menace. Then it dawned on me. "You're here to assess if I'm a threat." I cocked my head to one side. "You think you can ghost me?"

"I'd rather not have to find out."

"I have a century on you. Even with your recent shift, I'm not a soft target."

"You're older, slower, and can't cast."

"Last I checked, you weren't bulletproof." I shook my head. "It's *won't*, not can't. Hubris blinds those who claim to have the keenest sight."

"The arrogance of age must submit to be taught by youth."

"Burke. Not bad."

"Not as bad as quoting yourself."

"What can I say?" I shrugged. "I'm a legend in my own mind."

"I'm not here to fight you, Grey," he said, and I felt the energy around him dissipate. "At least not in this state."

"Then why are you here, Tristan?"

"You released an incredibly devastating spell in a

populated area, while wielding an artifact of unknown power, and you're a practicing dark mage," he said with a nod and extra levels of snootiness. "Forgive me if I'm a little concerned."

I looked down at the sword and noticed that the runic conduits had become darker and more pronounced. They had gone from fine hair-like filaments to thin cords of power that shimmered in the dim light.

"You're right," I said, getting out of bed and swaying as the meds made the room tilt. "It's not like I unleashed a void vortex or anything—twice. *That* would've been really dangerous, right?"

"There were…extenuating circumstances."

"Aren't there always?" I shot back. "Let me ask you something, Tristan."

He nodded. "Of course."

"If Roxanne were in mortal danger and the only way you could save her was to use dark magic—would you?"

"Yes," he said without hesitation. "If it was the only way."

"I hope you never have to make that choice," I said, my voice grim. "I wasn't able to save Jade."

"I know."

"Then you know I don't cast—so I'm not a practicing *anything* anymore. I'm a Night Warden. It's who I am—it's what I do."

"Not according to the Night Wardens."

"We're in the process of redefining my job description," I said. "There's been a slight miscommunication."

"Really?" He raised an eyebrow. "It was my impression they want you to retire—permanently."

"Just a difference of opinion. They think I should be dead and I disagree."

"What are you going to do?" He stood and pulled on his sleeves. "Are you going to complete the bond?"

"Not if I can help it."

"And if you can't?"

"I'll cross that bridge when I get to it." Pain was creeping up my face, even with the meds in my system.

"You can't sever the bond now—not without—"

"Killing myself, I know."

"If it overpowers you…"

"If I go full dark mage, take-over-the-world mental, I'll make sure you get the memo." I got back into bed because the floor was starting to sway again. "You'll be welcome to try and ghost me then."

"I apologize if I jumped to conclusions, Grey." He held out a hand and I took it. "I didn't mean to imply —"

"Hard to say no to the angry sorceress when she gets going, I know." The meds were making it hard to focus. "I'm serious, if anything goes wrong, you'll know. Until then, I have a rummer situation to deal with."

"I've heard," he said, serious. "Anything Simon and I could do to assist?"

"I'll give you a call if I need some buildings obliterated." I grabbed the sword and placed it on the side table next to me. "Other than that it's better if you stay out of the way—Night Wardens are a touchy bunch, and I already have them pissed off."

"I'd better get going." He opened the door. "Take care of yourself, Grey."

"Try not to blow up my city." I closed my eyes and felt myself drift.

TWENTY-THREE

"IT WAS AN entropic wave, Grey," Roxanne said with her arms crossed. "You know, the same kind of thing that's killing you?"

"And your solution was calling Tristan?" I snapped back, annoyed. "He came here ready to ghost me. Did you know that?"

"I called him."

I stared at her. "That's harsh—even for you."

"If you let yourself become corrupted by a dark blade, I'll *ghost* you myself," she said, her eyes fierce. "He was just in case I needed the assist."

I stole a glance at the sword. "You'll have to take a number. How did you know it was a dark blade?"

"Because Hades is going to give you a blade of love and light?" she scoffed. "Grow up, Grey. Hades is the god of the underworld. Everything he does is Dark— capital D. He makes shadows look bright."

She was right, I should've known better. Desperation makes men fools. I wanted to believe in a cure—even if it meant taking a dark blade from Hades.

"Koda?"

"Still alive, with no side effects." Roxanne looked at her clipboard. "She jumped in that thing you call a car and kept herself safe. How your car resisted the wave is another thing entirely."

"Runic phase shielding."

"On a car?" she said in disbelief. "But that would mean you took Ziller's theorem of quantum interstitial physics and—"

"Put it down, flipped it, and reversed it." I nodded, gesturing with my hand.

"You can't do that; it should tear the matter apart and shunt it out of phase."

"I didn't—Cecil had Elliott work on the Beast."

"The entropic wave you and that sword unleashed is still eating a hole in 6th Avenue," she said. "The Dark Council is bringing in Negomancers to deal with the containment, and they're going to be asking questions —the kind you don't want to answer."

"I need to get out of here before they show up." I grabbed the rest of my clothes. "They'll send someone here eventually."

"That wave could have killed you *and* Koda, Grey."

I squinted against the morning sun as she approached with a glass of water and pills. "I know what an entropic wave is, Rox," I said. "The last one I cast is slowly killing me every day. What is this? No more meds."

"These will remove the side effects of the meds from last night." She pushed the glass at me. "Trust me."

I took the pills reluctantly and downed them with a

gulp of water. My head started to clear immediately.

"What are those pills?"

"Pure caffeine, one thousand milligrams—each."

"This is almost as good as my super Deathwish coffee."

The raggedness from the meds vanished and my thoughts were clear. I had to make sure Cole kept some of those pills at The Dive to crush my migraines.

"What is it, Rox?"

"The rummers are getting worse," she said. "NYTF is reporting daylight attacks now."

"Shit," I muttered, putting on my shirt. The ink on my arms reacted to the sunlight, making the photoreactive runes on my skin shimmer and fade. "Where?"

"They were reported near Bryant Park."

"Any normals attacked?"

"None yet, but it's only a matter of time."

"Could you send some of those pills to Cole?" I put on my duster. "Where's Koda? Is she cleared to leave?"

"Pills to Cole—not on your life," she answered. "Koda, yes, next door. She tested negative for any effects the entropic wave, but when I tried to get a reading on her energy signature, there was an anomaly."

"Anomaly?" I knew this was coming. Koda's energy signature wasn't going to show up on any equipment.

"I couldn't get a reading on her." She frowned. "I may need to recalibrate the equipment. I've never seen anything like it."

"Could be the wave created some interference in the scan." I grabbed the sword and placed it in my duster pocket. It didn't jump this time, but I sensed the energy thrum in my hand. "I'll get Koda. You've wasted enough time on me. Get going Rox, I know you're busy."

"You and that coat always unnerve me." Roxanne observed as I put the sword away. "I didn't think of wave interference. I'll rerun the scans and factor for residual wave noise. I have to make my rounds. Please be safe out there, Grey."

"Can't guarantee safe, but I can do careful."

She gave me a quick hug and left the room. I stepped next door to get Koda.

"You can't let her scan me again." Koda's voice came from the corner. "If she does, she'll find out I'm a—"

She dropped her camouflage and appeared.

"That probably won't work on Roxanne."

"Worked on you *and* Corbel." She walked out of the room past me. "I'll take my chances. She surprised me with the scan last time, but I can't let her do it again."

"Not intending to—let's go." I motioned for her to join me. "We have rummers out during the day and a spell in the middle of the city to deal with. Maybe we can kill two birds with one hole."

TWENTY-FOUR

"THE RUMMERS WE didn't finish are still roaming the streets." I started the engine, and the Beast growled before settling into its familiar rumble.

"Are they attacking normals?"

"No." I swerved around traffic with the same nagging thought. "Something feels off about this. They're only going after magic-users."

"They're not exploding into rummer bits or attacking normals." I caught her looking at the runes on my hands as the sunlight hit them. "All of it feels off."

"What does *memento mori* mean?" She pointed at my right hand. The runic design was created to be indecipherable, but she read it with ease.

"You can read that?" I glanced down at the runes quickly. She nodded. Not even Jade had been able to read my runes. I'd have to remember to wear a shirt around Koda. "Remember that you have to die."

"Oh, I didn't mean to—" she started.

"Don't stress it," I said with a grunt. "It's not like

I'm going to forget anytime soon."

"Where are we headed?"

"We need to lead the rummers to 42nd Street." The Beast rumbled and roared as we sped uptown on 1st Avenue. "If they want magic-users, we can use the Dark Council to clean up the stragglers."

"Was he really there to ghost you?"

"Who? What are you talking about?"

"The other mage—the one with the English accent." She tapped the side of her ear. I had forgotten about the subdermal communicators. "He sounded serious and dangerous."

"He's both, and you shouldn't be listening in on conversations you aren't a part of."

"If he had tried to attack you, I would've stopped him." She looked out of the window. "Don't know if I can take him though."

"You can't, he's a battle mage—a good one." I glanced at her to drive the point home. "He would shred you before you got a chance to do your fandango."

"My what?"

"It's a fan dance that—nevermind." I pointed at her. "Don't even think of crossing him. He's usually cranky and in a bad mood."

"Must be a mage thing," she muttered under her breath. "Can _you_ take him?"

"He recently shifted, making him a serious threat, but,"—I said with a sly grin—"he really hates being called a wizard."

"So you can take him?"

"I don't intend on _ever_ finding out. Besides, he rarely

fights alone," I added, shaking away the image of my pushing Tristan's buttons by comparing him to the wizard who constantly burned down buildings in Chicago, or the one in Missouri who ran around with a werewolf. "His partner is what makes them a force to reckon with."

"I thought his partner was human?"

"His partner can't die. At least that's what I hear."

"He's immortal?" she said incredulously. "His partner is stronger than a god?"

"Even your ex-boss seems to respect them. I don't know if they're stronger or not, and I don't want to find out." I left out the part about Ebonsoul—Simon's blade matching the one in my duster. "Hold on."

She grabbed the door handle and braced herself as I pulled a tight left turn onto 39th Street and raced across town. I made a right on 6th Avenue and parked.

"The park is blocks from here." She looked around. "Why did you stop here?"

"Something or someone is controlling the rummers." I got out of the Beast and looked up and down the avenue. "We aren't here to fight them. I need to find who's pulling the strings."

"How do you plan on doing that?" she asked, slamming the door on her side—making me glad the windows were bulletproof Lexan.

"It's called the Beast—not the Heap." I gave her the stink-eye. "Would it be okay with you if we kept the doors attached?"

"Oh, sorry," she said with mock seriousness. "Do you think I hurt its feelings?"

"Would you like to walk back to The Dive?"

She raised her hands in surrender. "Sorry, really," she said with a smile. "I'll be gentle with her."

"Him, the Beast is a *him*."

"Not from where I'm standing." She put her hands on her hips. "Definitely female."

She crossed over to my side of the Beast and flicked her wrists, materializing her fans. "I don't see any rummers."

"If I can catch the melody, I can trace it back." I closed my eyes and let my senses expand.

"The what?"

"Active magic vibrates at a specific frequency." I turned slowly. "Ever since I cast the entropy spell, I can hear it, if it's strong enough."

"You can *hear* magic?"

"If you'd stop talking for a few seconds—wait, there." I opened my eyes and looked west on 39th Street. The sound was a subtle variation on the foghorn of destruction. "That way."

"What are you hearing?" she asked, keeping pace. "Is it like a whisper: 'this way to the dark magic' or something?"

"What? No." I looked at her. "It's tones and tastes," I said, automatically and regretted it the moment the words escaped my lips.

"Tastes? You can *taste* magic?" She burst into laughter and stopped walking.

"It's a side effect of not casting. The magic finds other senses to express its presence." I looked back at her and kept walking. "It's not that uncommon."

"You're serious?" She ran to catch up and stopped laughing when she saw my expression. "Sorry, I've just never heard of it before."

"I can hear the subtle tone of *your* magic."

"What is it?" she asked, curious. "What do I sound like?"

"Stand still and close your eyes." I stopped walking. "I can hear it now—it's coming through clearly."

"What do I sound like?"

I started walking away.

"You sound like an idiot who laughs at someone because they're different or exhibit a trait you're not familiar with."

She caught up a few seconds later. "Shit, Stryder, I'm sorry."

"I called you a freak—we're even." Her face darkened. I stopped walking. "We all carry baggage, all of us. I'm this way because of a spell, and you were born with yours. Not good or bad. Just different."

"I didn't mean—"

"Doesn't matter. We'll both do better next time." I pointed across Times Square and up Broadway. "Over there."

Whoever was casting the spell was in the subway.

TWENTY-FIVE

"THE TONE GETS stronger this way." I headed to the subway entrance, and she stopped. "They're in the subway—let's go."

"I can't." She took several steps back and I saw real fear in her eyes. "Not down there."

"What?" I looked down the stairs. "It's the subway. I know it's not the cleanest, but—"

"No," she said forcefully and stepped back even more. "I can't go down there. I can't go underground."

I took a deep breath, calmed myself, and kept my voice even. "You have a fear about being underground?"

She nodded. "It feels like the whole place is going to fall in on my head—suffocate me."

The tone was steady and strong, which meant we were close. I pushed it to the background as I spoke to her. Koda suffered from taphophobia—the fear of being buried alive. Which I could see if she were a miner. I didn't understand it, but I didn't need to—phobias are irrational.

"You worked for the god of the underworld." I pointed downstairs. "It's not that different."

"Underworld doesn't mean underground." She had a point. Hades usually sent Corbel to the underworld from what I heard. "Besides, you can't control that weapon."

"What does that have to do with anything?" I asked, trying not to agitate her further. "My control—or lack thereof—shouldn't affect you."

"There's a crater not four blocks from here because you used that... that *thing*." She took a few more steps back. "What happens if you use it down there and lose it again?"

"I won't."

"You won't use, it or lose control?"

"Both." I walked over to her. "It'll never leave my coat."

She stood frozen and focused on the entrance to the subway.

"I can't." She shook her head, clenching her jaw. "I can make sure no rummers follow you down."

She was reaching for a lifeline and I threw it to her.

"Fair enough." I placed a hand on her shoulder. "Thanks, I'll be right back."

I didn't bother explaining to her the futility of guarding one entrance. The 42nd Street-Times Square station was spread out over the center of the city. Rummers could swarm me from any number of entrances. Whoever chose it knew what they were doing.

"Stryder..." she said. I stopped and looked up from the stairway. She still looked tense. Her lips were drawn in a tight smile. Her body was rigid, a cable pulled tight —just shy of snapping. "Thanks for not laughing at me."

"Nothing to laugh at," I said. "If things get bad, head back to the Beast. You remember where it is?"

She nodded, and I headed down into the darkness. I needed to find a mage weaving a spell in one of the busiest stations in the city. I let my senses expand and listened. The tone was threaded with a sound I didn't recognize. It reminded me of nails on a chalkboard and set my teeth on edge.

I walked down the platform and dropped onto the tracks. I didn't expect to see a Transporter. They were shy, and whoever was weaving this spell would've scared them into hiding.

"Koda, can you hear me?" Cecil always provided top-of-the-line equipment. The communicators would be limited but they should function underground.

"Yes," she whispered. "Your big friend from The Dive just dropped off one of the Twins with the old mage."

They found Street.

"Can you stay out of sight?" I peered into the darkness. If Thing One was upstairs that meant Thing Two was down here somewhere, or vice versa. "Don't engage her alone, Koda."

"Not planning to," she said in a low voice. "Your mage friend looks banged up. He's covered in bruises. They're heading downstairs."

"Stay hidden," I said. "Her sister can't be too far away. Stay close in case I need backup."

"Backup?"

"Yes, you know that thing when you come and help me to not die? That backup?"

Silence.

"I'll make sure not to call you down here." I sighed and kept walking. "Stay hidden and I should be back soon."

I sensed the source of the tone farther down the tracks. It was between the stations in a large storage area. A bitter taste hit my tongue as I got closer. The additional saliva forced me to spit. "Great, now I'm Frank," I muttered.

Operational awareness was what allowed me to dodge the blast of black energy aimed at my head.

"Hello, Grey." It was one of the Twins. "I told Quinton you would come."

"What?" I glanced at the smoking wall next to me. "You're baiting me?"

She stood inside a circle. Dozens of black tendrils snaked out from her position and rose up and out of the station. The same black energy surrounded her and pulsed every few seconds. I narrowed my eyes and examined the tendrils. She was powering the rummers, but someone else had to be directing them.

"We need the vial."

"What vial?"

"I told him you would say that too." She smiled at me, and my stomach clenched. It was the checkmate smile. "Bring him," she yelled into the station.

I heard a scuffle, and another figure came into view. It was Street, followed by the other twin. He was pale and his eyes were unfocused. I saw the bruises and some of his fingers bent at unnatural angles, making it impossible for him to cast. His clothes were torn, and he looked dirtier than usual. She held a blade to Street's neck and dug it in deep enough to draw blood when I stepped closer to her.

"Please, come closer." She pressed the blade in again and drew more blood. "This old mage should be retired anyway."

I stopped walking.

"Let him go." I reached slowly into my pocket. I felt for the fake vial and pulled my hand out slowly—holding it between my thumb and forefinger. "This is what you want."

Behind me, the Twin in the circle muttered something under her breath, and more tendrils formed. I kept my eyes on the Twin in front of me. She stretched out a hand.

"Hand it here."

I opened my coat and made sure I could reach Fatebringer. The moment I gave her the vial, she would try to ghost Street. I had about three seconds.

"Give me the old man first."

She laughed at me. "How stupid do you think I am?" she said. "I give you the old man, and you blast me with your gun. No fucking way. Hand me the vial, or I hand him to you with his throat slit. He's dead either way—your choice."

I narrowed my eyes and examined Street. Something was wrong. I could see the same black tendrils forming in his chest. The Twin next to him laughed.

"What have you done?" I said, my voice a jagged growl.

"The vial—now." I placed the fake vial in her hand.

She grabbed it and shoved Street forward. I caught him as he fell into my arms. "You'd better hurry. Quinton gave him an extra dose. I wonder what happens when a psycho mage drinks Redrum?"

Her laughter followed me as I scooped up Street and ran out of the station. A few seconds later, I heard the muffled explosion. She must've opened the vial.

"Good for you, bitch," I said as I climbed the stairs.

TWENTY-SIX

THE BEAST RUMBLED outside as I reached the top of the stairs. I placed Street in the back. Koda moved over to the passenger side and strapped in.

"Will he make it?" she said, her voice tight as she looked in the back seat at a sweating and mumbling Street. "He looks bad."

"Quinton gave him Redrum." I pulled out my phone and speed dialed the only person I knew who could help.

"Are we going to Haven? He really needs to go to Haven."

I shook my head. "I don't think Rox can deal with this."

I sped across town until I hit the West Side Highway. I pulled a hard right and raced uptown. A voice answered a few seconds later.

"Hello, Grey." It was Aria.

"Street's in trouble." I jumped onto the Henry Hudson Parkway and blasted past traffic. "He's been given Redrum."

"How far away are you?"

"I'm on the Henry Hudson. Twenty minutes."

"Has he exhibited any symptoms?" she asked. "Do you know when he was given the drug and how much he was given?"

"No to all three." I swerved around several cars and pushed the Beast faster. I flipped a few switches and primed the nitrous oxide. Koda stared at me, wide-eyed. "He's not dying on my watch."

"I know this may be a long shot, Grey," Aria said after a pause, "do you have any of the Redrum he was given?"

"Yes, I think?"

"I'll get the rooms ready. Drive faster, Grey."

Aria hung up, and I glanced at Koda. "Hold on."

A flick of another switch, and the hydraulics lowered us to almost an inch off the road. Koda glanced at me as I hit the nitrous and the Beast roared. The velocity pushed us back in our seats as the needle on the speedometer arced to the right and stayed there.

"Hold on, Street." I white-knuckled the wheel and muttered under my breath. I dismissed the pain that shot up one side of my face.

"Stryder," Koda said, worried, "what are you doing?"

"Driving faster and saving his life."

The nitrous boost finished as I released the spell I had primed. The Beast suddenly became hundreds of pounds lighter as we sped up the parkway.

"You're casting?"

I clenched my jaw against the pain as runes flared inside the Beast. "We're almost there."

I pulled off the Henry Hudson and shot up the side

street that led to The Cloisters. The Wordweavers had taken ownership of the property from the Metropolitan Museum several decades back. They had kept the museum open, but sealed off one side and the top floors for themselves.

Aria stood at the entrance. She wore her usual white robe covered in silver runic brocade. Several assistants rolled out a gurney as I pulled up the cobblestone driveway.

I stopped the Beast, and she motioned to the weavers beside her to get Street. Koda bounded out and rushed to the driver's side as I stepped out. I promptly fell on my ass as someone pulled the road out from under my feet. Koda helped me stand unsteadily.

"Stryder, your nose." She pointed at my face. "You're bleeding."

"Give me a moment." I wiped my nose and came away with a bloody hand. "Shit, that can't be good."

"Grey, you need assistance," Aria said, looking back to the entrance of The Cloisters. Two more weavers came out with another gurney. "Take him to the runic dampener."

They nodded and wheeled me in.

The Cloisters contained architectural elements from four French medieval abbeys. What's not written in the tourism pamphlets is that these four abbeys were also ancient Wordweaver hubs of power. By combining, these four elements, the site became a nexus of power.

Wordweavers have existed as long as magic. Some say they were the first magic-users. Where Haven was a medical facility with magical applications, The Cloisters were a magical facility with medical applications.

Aria followed the gurney, and I peered at her as they wheeled me into a large room covered in runes. The symbols came to life with a chime of bells as we entered, and I immediately felt better. Koda looked around in surprise.

"What is this place?" she asked in wonder. "It's like a monastery for mages."

I nodded and regretted it as the room swam away from me. Aria approached and stared down at me. The silver brocade on her robe glimmered with power. Her long black hair cascaded behind her as she leaned over the gurney and gently tapped me on the forehead.

"You are one stubborn mage."

One of the assistants tended to my nose bleed and wiped the blood from my face, as Aria stood back and hovered behind him.

Normally stares didn't affect me, but hers was high on the unnerving scale. Her eyes, like my body, had been transformed by magic. Whatever ancient magic touched her left its mark by turning her irises and pupils white. She was the only weaver I had seen with this condition.

"Aria, I'm fine." I tried to sit up after the assistant was done and failed. I wasn't fine.

"Do I need to strap you down?"

I slowly shook my head. "The Redrum—"

"I can get it," she said and held a hand over my duster. The vial appeared in her hand a second later, and she handed it over to the assistant. "Analyze and work up an antidote now. Administer the antidote to the patient in Emergency."

"Is Street going to be okay?" I saw the assistant run

out with the vial. "He looked bad in the car."

"Too soon to tell," she answered. "What happened?"

I explained what was going on with the UV-resistant rummers and the new strain of Redrum. I told her my thoughts about Lyrra being behind this somehow.

"She was always ambitious, but this plan—turning homeless into rummers—seems beyond her."

"She always wanted to control the Night Wardens," I said. "Felt they were going soft. Not upholding the law."

Aria shook her head. "Lyrra doesn't possess the knowledge to alter the genetic structure of vampire blood to this degree, much less make it a catalyst for UV resistance."

"Who does?" I asked. "What am I looking for? What kind of mage knows how to do this?"

"You're not looking for just a mage." She glanced at Koda. "Is this your new partner?"

Koda was still looking around in awe at the rune work inscribed on all the surfaces of the room. I was about to make a comment when I remembered her reluctance to go underground. The question wasn't a deflection. Aria wanted to know how much she could share.

"Yes—in training." Koda raised an eyebrow at me. "We have a few things to work out, but she's starting to learn."

"You're looking for a Smith—an Exiled."

"Are you sure?" My voice betrayed my confusion. "I thought all the Smiths were here?"

Aria shook her head. "Some Wordweavers get tempted to live a life of material wealth and gain.

Those that do are banned from the grounds, stripped of power, and cast out."

"Exiled," Koda said. "Isn't that a little harsh?"

"Which part?" Aria answered, her voice holding a slight edge. "The part where we prevent them from accessing our libraries full of ancient magical knowledge, or the part where we reduce their power to cause harm, and cast them out so they don't corrupt the others?"

"Neither," I interrupted before Koda said something dangerous. "Where would I find an Exiled Smith?"

"Ellis Island, but they have left it since the incident with the Blood Hunters."

"I heard that's where Nick lost his head."

"Literally." She waved a hand over my duster again, narrowed her eyes at me, and spoke under her breath.

"I need to find the Exiled, Aria."

She whispered something unintelligible and the sword materialized next to me on the gurney.

"What you *need* to do is tell me about this sword, Grey."

I should've known better than to bring it near her.

TWENTY-SEVEN

"IT'S NOTHING." I sat up and grabbed the sword before she could unsheathe it. "Just a trinket."

"A trinket?" She spoke in a language I didn't understand, and the sword leaped out of the scabbard into her hand. "This is no trinket—try again."

What she did was amazing for several reasons. We were in a runic dampening room, which meant all magic was suppressed. It helped me recover from the effects of the spell killing me. It also should've limited her magic from functioning.

She had used magic several times with no apparent effort. It meant that her level of magic was greater than the dampening effect of the room. I didn't want a pissed-off Wordweaver, so I told her what I knew about the sword—including the part about Hades.

"Why would he give you this sword?" She turned the blade in her hand. The runes shimmered dimly. "This weapon is designed to undo the supernatural. It puts him at risk."

"Maybe he gave it to me from the goodness of his

heart?"

"Don't be naïve, Grey, he's an old god. They always have an ulterior motive—him more than most."

"I told him," Koda said. "Hades never shows his real hand."

"He said it could stop the spell killing me." I looked at her. "I only have to bond with it and be its host."

"You're practically bonded," she said. "Why haven't you finished the process?"

"No! I refuse to be a host to some bloodthirsty psycho sword." I extended the scabbard, and she sheathed the sword. "Not now—not ever."

"I don't think I was being clear." Aria shook her head. "You're practically bonded. You *must* finish the process before it siphons the life from you."

"What do you mean 'siphons the life' from me?" I asked, alarmed. "I'm not bonded to it."

She pointed at the sword. "Do you see the conduits?"

"Yes, I saw the small strands before."

"Look again. Do they look like small strands now?"

I expanded my senses and saw nothing.

"The room must be blocking my ability." I looked up at her. "I don't see anything."

She whispered under her breath again and all of the runes in the room went dark.

"Try now."

I looked at the sword. A large strand about the size of my wrist connected me to the sword. I could see the strand pulse slowly.

"What the hell is that?" I pointed at the strand that gave off black energy, reminding me of the tendrils in the subway.

"Have you used this weapon in combat?" Aria stared at me, and I saw no point in lying again.

"He fought ogres and rummers with it," Koda answered. "Then he lost his mind."

"Excuse me?" Aria said. "What occurred?"

"Nothing." I shifted in the gurney, uncomfortable. "It siphoned power into me and I wasn't ready—that's all."

"That's not all," Koda added. "He was howling like a maniac, and he slashed himself several times as he swung that thing around. This was after he almost buried us under a truck as he drove."

"You cut yourself—with the blade?" Aria asked slowly. "Do you remember this, Grey?"

"I don't recall cutting—"

"I saw it. Saw you." Koda stared me down. "You lost your mind, swung that thing around, and cut yourself a few times."

I remembered the bandages in Haven, but I thought they were rummer injuries.

"Hades wasn't lying," Aria said, narrowing her eyes at me. "That sword *can* stop the entropic dissolution— *if* you bond to it. Otherwise it's just going to kill you faster every time you use it."

I looked at Koda and saw her try to hide the concern on her face. Roxanne's words came back to me, *Now it's not just your life, is it?* If I let the sword ghost me, there were people who would be vulnerable. People close to me who would die.

"I'm not going to be its host," I said, my voice grim. "That never ends well."

Aria nodded. "As long as you know the consequences of your actions." She spoke again, and the runes came to life. "I can't force you—no one can."

"How long?" I looked down at the sword. "How long before it's too late?"

"At the rate it's siphoning from you, if you don't cast, I'd say six months, maybe a year."

"And if I cast?" I asked, not really wanting the answer.

"There are several variables—" she started.

A mage spoke this way when what they really meant was: "You're fucked."

"Don't magespeak me, Aria," I said, getting off the gurney. The room had reversed the effects of the casting and I felt like roadkill, my usual state. "Just tell me how long."

"It has your blood—the bond is now irreversible," she whispered, waving a hand and speaking under her breath. Light orange tendrils flowed from her fingers into me. They formed a latticework of energy that wrapped itself around me and disappeared. "If you keep your casting to the minor spells—and by minor, I mean little to no energy required—you have about three months."

"Three months to a year." I placed the sword in my duster. "Plenty of time to do what needs to be done."

"Stryder," Koda said, "we could call the NYTF or the Dark Council. Let them handle this."

"They can't." I checked Fatebringer and tightened the holster. "The NYTF isn't equipped and the Dark Council won't touch the Night Wardens."

"What about the mage and his immortal friend?"

"I'd rather keep the city in one piece, thank you." I turned to Aria. "I need a few things, but first, I want to see Street."

"He's in Emergency," she said, heading to the door. "I have to tend to a few things. Why don't you go on ahead, and I'll meet you there."

The quiet corridors of The Cloisters vibrated with a low hum. The ambient magic was old, powerful, and felt like honey with a hint of lemon. This wasn't the first time I had walked in with a life hanging in the balance.

"Is she strong?" Koda asked next to me. "She seems to have a lot of power. Especially the way she pulled out the sword."

"Aria is a Wordweaver." I remembered her words about my casting. "Wordweavers reframe reality with their thoughts and words. Yes—she is powerful. Powerful enough to cast in there."

I pointed behind us to the runic dampener room.

"Why do you do it?" Koda said. "Why do you care? You could just walk away, not get involved. Why risk your life?"

"It's the right thing to do." I examined the book in my hands

"The Wardens removed you from their ranks, but you still go out on patrol."

"I guess I'm just too stubborn and set in my ways to do anything else," I said. "Besides, I don't need *their* permission."

"You could just stop," she said. "No one is forcing you to risk your life every night."

"Someone has to be there to stop the monsters in

the night." I turned the book, causing the runes to activate. "Someone has to stand for those who can't."

"And that virtuous person is you?"

"No," I said with a grim laugh. "I'm just doing this until he or she shows up. Any more questions? I really need to look into this."

"Is Aria stronger than a mage?" she asked as we turned down a corridor. The Cloisters contained a labyrinth of passageways that all looked the same to the untrained eye. If you didn't know where you were going, you never got there. It was part defensive strategy and part sadistic torture.

Anyone trying to invade would find themselves hopelessly lost, roaming the corridors endlessly. Whoever designed this part of The Cloisters had a twisted sense of humor. We turned at another corridor and stepped into the Emergency area.

"Mages and Wordweavers both manipulate energy to affect the world around them." I looked around to see if Street was in any of the beds. "Mages use gestures, runes, and the occasional catalyst to create magic."

"What about Wordweavers?"

"Wordweavers use thought and words." I walked farther into the Emergency ward. "Thought is pure energy. Every thought you have, have ever had, and ever will have is creative. Aria can create and cast ten spells before I finish one, maybe two if I'm really fast."

"That's insane." I stopped us at the rear of the ward. We stepped out and turned right. Another larger area had occupied beds, with assistants walking in the midst of them.

"What's insane is trying to fight a wordweaver." I

saw Street and headed for his bed. "It's usually a short fight, with only the Wordweaver walking away and no —I can't take her—in case you were wondering."

"I wasn't," Koda answered. "She looked like she could kick your ass all over this mage monastery."

"Your vote of confidence in my ability is breathtaking." I pulled her to the side before we approached Street. "I don't know if he's lucid or not. He may not know who I am—his mind does that sometimes. Don't do anything to upset him."

She nodded and hung back a few paces as we approached his bed. He looked at me with a smile. I sighed in relief at the recognition.

"Hey, Street." I grabbed his hand and gave it a gentle squeeze. "You're looking better."

"Stop bullshitting me, boy," he said with a grin and grew serious. "I look like shit, and you're in for a world of pain."

TWENTY-EIGHT

"WHAT ARE YOU talking about?" I asked.

"Bastards tried to turn me into one of those zombie vamps—rummers, you call them." He waved his hands around. "But it's worse. Did I give you the vial? Can't remember my own name some days."

"I got it, thanks." I nodded. "How is it worse?" I dreaded his answer.

"You have a new partner." He craned his neck around me to get a better look at Koda. "Where are your manners?"

"Street, this is Koda. Koda this is—"

"She is a cipher," he said, narrowing his eyes at me. "And you've been casting again." He gently touched the back of my hand. "What have I told you about casting, Grey?"

"That it's bad for my health," I replied. "I didn't have a choice. Things out there are getting bad."

"One of your old crew, Lyrra, is out there creating an army of those rummer things." He looked away for a few seconds. "She's giving them this new drug, forcing them to take it. Took some of my friends too. She's going after street people. Everyone thinks we're trash, worthless, invisible. She's taking them."

"I know," I said, barely containing the anger. "I'll find her and stop her."

"You can't." He squeezed my hand. "Promise me you won't go out there, Grey."

"I can't," I said. "Someone needs to stop her."

"Doesn't need to be you," he said. "Call the Council or that new and improved police force they have that handles the supernatural activities."

"The NYTF?"

"Them—let them handle it."

"In all your years in the street, have you ever seen them resolve anything but the end-of-world problems?" I answered and placed his hands on his lap. "They don't care about the old mage in the park being chased, or the woman being attacked by werewolves. That was always the Night Wardens."

"She has ogres, Grey." He looked me in the eyes and I could see the fear. "Big ones that move fast like you or me. I don't know how she did it. Ogres usually move real slow, but these…She's building an army, Grey. You need to stay away."

"I will," I said and patted his hands. I could tell he was getting agitated and didn't want him to lapse into his paranoia. "I'll make sure to stay away from them."

"Promise me."

"Tell me how you got the vial," I said. "Where did you get it?"

He looked off into the distance, and I thought I had lost him. I was about to step away when he snapped back.

"The park." His voice was a whisper, and he looked around furtively. "She's in Shadow Helm—the old Night Warden Keep in the park."

"I thought that was closed down and destroyed?"

"It was, but not the underground levels," he answered rapidly. I could see one of the assistants approach. I held him off with a subtle gesture. "She's down there, making the army. We went down there to sleep, I saw them, and she chased me. Almost got me too. Then I grabbed a vial. I knew it was the bad blood. That's when I saw the ogres and felt something else—something bad."

"She's giving the ogres the bad blood?"

"All of them." He nodded. "She's making more monsters down there—something worse than ogres. You can't go down there, Grey. They'll get you too."

The assistant approached again and this time I stepped back. He whispered some words, and I could sense the gentle magic falling on Street. In a few seconds, he was asleep. Aria stepped in behind me.

"You heard?" I turned to face her. "Is that where they are?"

"You can't go in there." She stepped over to the bed and placed a hand on Street's chest. He began breathing deeply. "They almost turned him."

"Then you know where I'm going." I looked down at Street. "I have to stop them."

She turned to face me, and I heard the high-pitched tone.

"If you go down there with that sword siphoning your energy and your condition, you're not coming back out."

"I can control this." I tapped the butt of my gun. "I don't need to use the sword when I have Fatebringer."

"Oh?" Aria extended a hand and raised an eyebrow. "Then you won't mind leaving the sword here."

"You cannot leave me, mage," Izanami said as I pulled out the sword. "I advise against this."

"The hell I can't." I handed the sword to Aria. "You don't get to tell me what to do."

"It communicates with you?" Aria looked down at the sword. "How long has this been happening?"

"Long enough to be aggravating." I pulled my duster closed. "See? Sword no longer in possession. No negative side-effects."

"You haven't tried to leave—yet," Aria said her face grim. "What is the weapon's name?"

"Izanami. At least that's what it told me."

Aria nodded and motioned me on. "Well, I must have been mistaken," she said. "Feel free to leave whenever you're ready—you know the way out. Don't let me keep you from storming the park and taking down Lyrra and her army."

I looked at Street again and left the Emergency area with Koda next to me.

"Is that a good idea?" she asked as we walked. "I mean, I'm not a fan of you losing your mind, but we're going up against Night Wardens, ogres and who knows how many rummers. We could use all the help we can get."

"What was the first thing I told you?" I snapped. The temperature was rising. We must have been close to a furnace. I felt heat all around me.

"It's rude to grab a man's weapon without permission," she said, her face serious. She raised a hand in surrender when I glared at her. "If I touch your gun again, you'll shoot me yourself?"

"About trust—what did I tell you about trust?" I leaned against the wall. It was getting hard to catch my breath. "Who can you trust?"

"You're not looking too good, Stryder."

"I'm fine." I wiped the sweat away from my eyes. "Let's get out of here."

I took a few steps and found my legs heavy. My vision tunneled in and I had to stop.

"Are you lost?" Aria said as she approached us. "I can lead you out if you need help."

"It's the bond, isn't it?" I stared at her as she held the sword in front of her. "It's doing this."

"Until you complete the process, the bond is parasitic." She handed me the sword, and the heat around me dissipated. "Once you complete the bond, it becomes symbiotic."

"Fuck," I said with a grunt and stared at Koda. "I'm going to kill your ex-boss next chance I get."

"Would you like to complete the process now?" Aria asked as I walked away. "I can help facilitate the bonding."

I put the sword in my coat, walking to the exit.

"No," I growled at her. "I have a Night Warden to kill. If I'm still alive after that, we'll talk."

TWENTY-NINE

"DO WE HAVE a plan?" Koda asked as I drove downtown on the Henry Hudson. "Or are we just going to rush in all badass and take as many as we can before they shred us?"

"I'm not planning on being ghosted today—not by a sword or by Lyrra," I answered. "We need to go to The Dive and get some things. We'll hit the park tonight."

"So this is my last day." Koda looked out the window. "At least it wasn't boring."

"What the hell are you talking about—last day?"

"If it's just going to be the two of us, we're going in blind," she said, raising her voice. "We don't know how many there are. How many of them are mages, ogres, rummers, or whatever else she has waiting for us?"

"We'll know that before we get to the park."

"Plus, are you in a hurry to die?" she shot back. "I get it. Your life sucks and you want to end it all. That doesn't mean I want to join you in a suicide run."

"There's going to be dying tonight—lots of it," I said. "Just not by us."

"Street said this place is underground." she shivered. "I can't help you if we have to go *underground*, Stryder."

"I'll make sure there's plenty of action above ground," I said with a tight smile. "Wouldn't want you to get bored."

I pulled up to the front of The Dive and let the Beast rumble for a few seconds before turning off the engine. I let my senses expand and felt the new defenses push up against my probing. General Java had used active runes instead of passive defenses.

If I kept probing, the runes would home in on my location and reward me with runic equivalent of a punch to the face. I kept pushing until I felt the defenses actively seek me out, then I stopped. They would only target someone actively trying to penetrate the perimeter.

I crossed the threshold and felt a wave of energy wash over me. I examined the doorframe but didn't see any runes. Several of the regulars were seated at the bar and around tables in the center of the floor. Koda walked in behind me and gasped.

"What was that?" she said, surprised.

"It seems some of the new defenses are designed to bar entry if needed," I answered, heading to the bar where Cole stood. "What you felt was your energy signature being stored."

"How can it store something I don't—?"

"Even nothing can be something," I said, cutting her off. I didn't want anyone else to know she was a cipher just yet.

"I meant, I'm not a mage or magic-user," she said, keeping her voice low as she noticed several of the patrons perk up at our conversation.

"You're not normal either." I grabbed Cole's attention. "Deathwish, something healthy for her, and Frank—in that order."

"He's in the training area. The ink you call coffee will be up in five." Cole grabbed my mug from the rack and placed it on the counter. "You have a guest."

I nodded and took the stairs to the second level. Koda trailed behind me silently.

"Step back. If this is who I think it is, you don't want to be in the way."

She stepped back and flicked her wrist, materializing a fan.

I placed my hand next to the door, unlocking it. Nothing came barreling at me, which I took as a good sign.

"Frank?" I said into the room before stepping across the threshold. I let my senses expand and felt out the room—nothing. I was about to go downstairs and tell Cole no one was on the training level when I heard the tingle of bells. I ducked, and a short staff crashed into the door at the same height as my head.

I rolled to the side, avoiding another staff strike. I raised my arm and duster to deflect a barrage of strikes as I drew Fatebringer with my opposite hand.

"Don't kill him, Yat," I heard Frank say. "He still owes me money."

"Was this your idea?" I stared at Frank. "If it is, I'm shooting you first."

"Hello, Grey," said Yat. "You're looking well for a dead man."

"Dying, not dead." I peeked over the sleeve of my

duster. "Are we done or do I need to start shooting?"

I looked over at the thin older man holding a staff and smiling at me. He was nearly my height, and his slight build hid his immense strength. The last time I saw him, he wore his hair long. Now it was cropped short—a white crown glimmering in the subtle light of the room. His eyes were still the same: deep, dark, and unreadable.

He retracted the staff and held out a hand, which I took.

"It has been some time," he said. "How are you?"

"I did my part." Frank shook his head and sent sparks flying everywhere. "Unlike him, you'll know where to find me." He crackled one last time, shook his tail, and disappeared.

"He's still as pleasant as ever, I see." Yat looked around the training area. "You've kept the space as I instructed, thank you."

"Don't get to use it as much as I'd like." I flicked the switches, turning on all the lights. "Your room is in the back, kitchen on the side and everything is stocked."

Yat nodded. "Where is this student Frank kept mentioning?" I knew he had noticed Koda, probably before we even reached the second floor. No one ever snuck up on Yat. "He informs me she is quite skilled."

I gestured with a head motion and his eyes slid to the side.

"Before you light up her life with pain, you and I need to talk." I turned to Koda. "Give us a few minutes. Why don't you get your gear ready for tonight."

Koda looked at Yat in silence. I didn't know if it was

recognition or surprise at the ferocity of his attack.

"Hello? Earth to space cadet?" I snapped a finger and she focused on me, shaking her head. "Upstairs prep then downstairs food. Don't crush Frank. Got it?"

"Got it." She stepped out of the room while still looking at Yat. I closed the door and made sure it was secure. I let my senses expand and felt her particular 'nothingness' go upstairs.

"She is very much like my brother." Yat placed the staff on the rack near the wall. "She is strong, stronger than he was."

"She's something else with those fans."

"I'm not staying, Grey."

"Excuse me?" I said, surprised. "There's plenty of space. You know that."

He raised a hand to stop me. "It's too dangerous for various reasons." He sat on one of the benches. "In time, she would make the connection."

"You're her family; you should be close, protecting her." I took off my duster and hung it on a hook near the door. "That's what family does, protects each other."

"She doesn't need protecting—she needs guidance." He looked off into the distance. "I have kept away *because* I've been protecting her. The forces after me would kill her if they found out her connection to me."

"Still?" I asked.

"Always," he said, his voice grim. "There's no statute of limitation on revenge."

"Yat, if I don't make it tonight," I said, "Hades will come for her."

"I will make sure she is cared for." He stared at me.

"You've grown worse. What caused it?"

"It's complicated," I said. "Hades is involved."

"How long?"

"Three months to a year." I looked away for a second. "Unless I take his offer."

"I trust you will make the right choice."

"He read me and then pulled me in like a rank amateur." I shook my head in frustration. "And I fell for it. Predictable."

"Then don't be predictable," Yat said with small smile. "He is quite the spider, with his hands touching every strand. Don't be the fly."

"Easier said than done." I unholstered Fatebringer. "His reach is impressive."

"Even a god has his limits." He dusted off one sleeve and stood blading his body. "Koda will not return to him, no matter the outcome of your encounter tonight."

"Who's going to train her with those fans?"

"You." He pointed at my chest. "You're dying, not dead. May as well make productive use of your time. Let's converse, and then I will know if I must find another."

I stepped to the center of floor. I knew why he came. It wasn't to have this chat. It was to have one of his *true conversations*, as he called them.

"You didn't have to come here, we could've spoken over the phone."

"The truest conversation is engaged in combat—you know this."

"I don't expect to see another sunrise."

"You will, and you must, Dragonfly," he said quietly,

and grew serious. "Your life is not yours any longer. You never understood that—even with Jade."

The words stung, but he was right. I bladed my body, turning to the side to present a small profile.

He stepped in thrusting forward with a fist. I twisted to the side. I felt the displaced air as he opened his hand and sliced across. I ducked under the knifehand and stepped in with a palm strike aimed at his chest.

He stepped back, causing me to miss by a fraction of an inch. As I closed the distance he wrapped his arm around mine locking it in place. He dropped his weight to break the joint. I shoved forward, bending my elbow before he could shatter the joint.

He released my arm, and snaked his hand to my neck. Tucking my chin, I turned my body and thrust a spearhand at his throat, stopping just short and disrupting his momentum.

He released me and stepped back with a short bow. I did the same.

"I still think you should train her," I said, turning at the knock at the door. "That's Cole with my Deathwish."

I opened the door and Cole handed me a large mug of black javambrosia before heading downstairs again. I held the cup to my nose for a few seconds before taking a sip of liquid paradise.

"I can't believe you still drink that," he said and scrunched his nose at the aroma. "Does it still help?"

"Dulls the headaches and generally makes me mildly anti-social."

"As opposed to completely?" he said with a slight smile. "You will train Koda. She needs to learn from someone—"

"Ruthless?"

"I was going to say accomplished," he finished. "You were always better at close-quarter combat, Dragonfly. Her fans are the ultimate short-range weapon, and Master Mushin passed on the style to you."

"To us," I corrected. "He passed it on to *us*."

"And yet you bear the title and the crest."

"I'm just waiting for you to get your act together and claim the *menkyo kaiden*." I sipped my coffee. "That way you can be the successor."

He shook his head. "Won't happen in this lifetime or the next. We make our choices and live with them. This is my path now. Yours, it seems, is to keep being a Night Warden."

"Not according to them," I said as I opened the door. "Going to have a violent conversation with some Night Wardens tonight."

"I'm grateful I'm not facing you this evening," Yat said, rubbing his forearms. "Do you want my advice?"

"I'm listening." I sat on the bench and drank more coffee. My forearms screamed at me from his repeated blows, but I wasn't going to let him know that.

"You need to take care of those around you, and this place." He gestured to the building around us. "This is still known as the oasis in the midst of the madness."

"You're saying bond with the thing." I stared at him hard. "You know me. My track record with commitment is stupendously bad."

"I'm saying choose life." He extended his arm and the staff rushed into it. "You have more at stake than you know. This isn't just about you. Who will keep the streets safe if you're gone?"

I didn't have an answer for him.

"Thank you for coming." I extended a hand. "I know this was a risk for you."

"Don't send your lizard for me again." He nodded and we clasped forearms. "I have to go. Next time we will have a longer conversation."

"I would enjoy that, Yat," I said as he stepped back and traced his staff along the floor, creating a golden circle of runes. "Be light in the shadow."

"And shadow in the light," he answered and stepped in to the circle and disappeared.

I grabbed my duster and headed downstairs.

THIRTY

SEVERAL PATRONS WERE seated around the floor, having drinks and keeping mostly to themselves. At the bar, Cole had just served some drinks. Frank and Koda looked up when I came down the stairs.

I motioned to Cole with my chin. He pressed a section under the bar, creating a quiet zone. None of the patrons ever noticed, and if they did, it never bothered them that it was always quiet at the bar even when The Dive was full.

"What's this I hear about storming Shadow Helm?" Frank asked as I approached the bar. I glanced over at Koda. "It's true? When are we leaving?"

Frank's tail started doing the seismic tango. I slid my mug along the bar. Cole reached out without looking, removed it, and placed it in the sink in one smooth motion.

"*We* aren't leaving anywhere."

"Are you taking fan-girl?" he asked and spit. His tail was still waving about. Cole grabbed a towel and put out the flames. "She's not exactly battle ready. No offense, but you certainly don't inspire confidence with those things, unless you plan on keeping them cool and —"

I noticed liquid on the bar and was about to ask Cole when Frank went rigid and stopped midsentence. He looked down at the liquid pooled around his feet.

"Oh, shit," I heard Cole whisper behind the bar.

"Grey, this is—" he muttered and looked up at me. The whites of his reptilian eyes glowed with power.

Koda looked around, confused. "What happened?"

"Everybody, down!" I yelled as I jumped over the bar and pulled Koda with me. I heard several of the tables being overturned as chairs scraped the floor. The sounds of bodies thudding against the floor filled the space. I kept my back to Frank as an intensifying crackling sound ripped through The Dive, followed closely by a thunderclap. This was followed by the sound of shattering glass and a couple of muffled car alarms.

In the stunned silence that followed, punctuated by the occasional crunching noise, I stood slowly and did a quick check of the customers. Everyone seemed to be fine but shaken. I brushed off the glass from my shoulders and surveyed the damage. I held out an open palm near the now sagging and seemingly exhausted Frank, who wearily dragged himself into it and slumped down.

"What the hell was that?" Koda asked from behind the bar.

"That was Frank," I said. "Now you know why we keep the alcohol behind Lexan and not in front of a mirror. Excuse me a sec."

I gently carried Frank to one of the back rooms for him to shake it off. "Sorry, Grey," he slurred. "I should've watched where I put me feet."

"Don't worry about it, dragon." I shifted him to my other hand as I opened the door to the rear guest quarters. "Everyone has a drink they can't handle—even you."

I paused for a second as he rocked back and forth and nodded. "Having said that, I'll ask Cole not to stock the Fireball Whisky. Just as a safety precaution."

He nodded again and passed out.

I placed him on the bed and stepped outside. Everyone had fixed the tables and were getting their drinks refilled. I headed to the bar.

"Cole, let him sleep it off and remove the Fireball." I pointed at the bottle. "We don't need any more dragon lightning in here. Don't let him out of your sight when he comes to."

Cole grabbed the bottle and put it under the bar. I examined the extent of the strike and saw that it was contained to the bar. Java had done a good job with the defensive runes. The last time Frank unleashed a strike, we were dealing with fires and structural damage.

"Are we really just going to storm this Shadow Helm on our own?" I heard the tinge of fear in Koda's voice. "Wouldn't it be better to call the NYTF at least?"

"What did I tell you?" I pulled out my phone and pressed a speed dial. "No one's got your six."

"So we're going to die," she said, her voice tight. "This is insane."

"I may be insane, but I'm not suicidal."

The call connected.

"Are you on your way in again?" Rox said with a sigh. "Should I prep your usual room?"

"Not yet." I paused for a few seconds. "I need a favor."

"You need a what?" she asked, surprise evident in her voice. "Mr. 'I work alone and I'm too badass to ask for help' is asking for a favor?"

"Yes, I'm attacking the lower levels of Shadow Helm tonight," I said, my voice tight. "I need your destructive duo and their devil dog. Can you call them?"

"Grey," Roxanne answered, sounding serious, "Shadow Helm was destroyed. The lower levels are sealed. There's nothing down there."

"Lyrra and her renegade Night Wardens are down there, along with who knows how many rummers and Redrum ogres."

"Redrum ogres?"

"I'll meet them at the 86th Street entrance," I said. "Eleven sharp. By that time the streets will be clear. If they're late, I go in without them."

"If you're right, this is suicide, Grey," she said. "Call the NYTF or the Dark Council."

"This is Night Warden business," I answered. "You know the NYTF and Council will show up after everything is done, if they show up at all."

"I don't know if Tristan and Simon will be enough," she said. "You're storming what I assume to be a fortified position."

"Can you call them?"

"Are you sure you want Tristan there?" she asked. "You two don't exactly get along."

"He may be a royal pain, but he's good at

destruction." I glanced at Koda. "Right now I can use all the firepower I can get. Call him."

"Did you bond to the sword?"

"No, and I don't intend to."

"I'll call him and prep the room." She hung up.

I looked at Cole and nodded.

"Ghost Protocol?" he asked.

"You don't hear from me in two days max—Ghost Protocol and have Cecil pick up the Beast for decommissioning."

"I'll get on it now." He nodded and left the bar, heading to the back room to prep.

"You have everything you need?" I looked at Koda. "I don't want to hear you left a fan behind or something."

"Funny. What's Ghost Protocol?"

I headed to the door and she kept pace. The Beast rumbled as I started the engine.

"Exactly what it sounds like." I closed my eyes and let the purr of the engine wash over me. "If I don't show up or contact Cole in two days, and he ghosts The Dive and everything in it."

THIRTY-ONE

WE ARRIVED AT 86th Street with thirty minutes to spare. I stepped out of the Beast and checked Fatebringer. I had ten speed loaders filled with an assortment of rounds but heavy on the negation. I faced the street as Koda walked to the wall that bordered Central Park.

"Do you think they'll come?" She looked down Central Park West. The traffic was light. "I don't think I would if I were them."

"Even if we get Tea and Crumpets, it'll be better than just us."

"You don't like him, do you?" she asked.

"I respect him—I don't have to like him." I looked up at her. "If things go south, and they usually do, you get your ass out of the park before you get ghosted."

"But I—"she started and I glared at her hard, cutting her off.

"Don't sass me." I holstered Fatebringer. "You find yourself in over your head, you run to safety. Clear?"

"Got it," she muttered under her breath. "What if

you get in trouble?"

"I'll get myself out—or I won't." I felt the circle before I saw it. "We have company."

Koda looked around. "Where? I don't see anyone?"

An orange circle formed a few feet away from us. I only sensed one signature, but it was impressive. Tristan must have shifted more than one level to register this strong.

A few seconds later, Tristan stepped from the circle and walked to us. He was dressed in his usual dark suit. I swear it's like a uniform with some mages.

"Where's your partner and his hound?"

"Simon and his creature are following up on leads in a current case." He pulled on his sleeve as he looked into the park. "Roxanne insisted that you needed *help*?"

"I'm never going to live this down."

"Not to worry," he said with a nod and tapped the side of his head. "You know us mages—memories like sieves."

"Hilarious. All the mages I know—present company included—are about as funny as a funeral."

"I wasn't being funny," he said with a serious look.

"Right. Koda is topside." I glanced quickly her way and she nodded. "She makes sure nothing follows us in. You and me go in and erase everything in there that's not a Night Warden."

"This new strain of Redrum… is it—?"

"Fatal? Yes." I nodded. "Once they're turned there's no antidote. I almost lost a close friend to it today. It has to be caught before the actual turning. Once they're rummers, it's too late."

"What are we facing?" He pulled out a roll of paper

from an inside pocket and smoothed it out on the top of the low wall that surrounded the park. It was a plan of the underground levels of Shadow Helm.

"Where did you get that?" I looked at the plans, and they seemed accurate. "Only Night Wardens have access to those plans."

"Night Wardens and Directors of the NYTF, it seems," he said. "Who, by the way, know you're here tonight poking a hornet's nest."

"Should I wait until the NYTF decides it's time to shut down Lyrra and her army?"

"Only if you wish to wait a lifetime," he answered. "I'm letting you know who the scapegoat will be if this goes horribly wrong, and who will take the credit if it doesn't."

"How many more homeless have to die before it becomes an issue?" I asked, getting angry. "How many more attacks before they take action?"

"Isn't that what we're here to do—shut them down?" he inquired calmly and pointed at the plans. "Show me what I'm looking at. How do we get in and — more importantly—out?"

"We can use this tunnel system." I traced a finger along the plan. "The underground has three levels, with the deepest being the most complex. If Lyrra is down there, she'll be on the lowest level. I have a secret way in."

"The third level, which I can presume is the most fortified?" he said, pointing to the third level on the plans. "Runic defenses?"

"None that would be active, but she's dangerous, so I wouldn't discount them."

"I'll approach as if they're in place." He rolled up the plans, putting them in a pocket. "How many rummers?"

"I don't know." I looked into the darkness of the park. "She's been taking people off the street and forcing this new Redrum into them."

"Rummers unknown, fine." He adjusted his jacket. "What about these Redrum ogres Roxanne mentioned?"

"Ogres." I nodded. "Like your regular ogres—only smarter, with insane reflexes, and fast moving. These aren't the hulking ogres you're used to."

"So ogres on Redrum have increased lethality." He rubbed his chin. "Night Wardens are mages as well, yes?"

"Only the higher positions, rank and file are closer to apprentices," I said. "She has three that I know of, not including Lyrra herself, Quinton and the Twins."

"I've heard of this trio—nothing good," he said. "Night Warden death squad of some sort."

I nodded. "Assassins—and good at what they do." I nodded. "The Twins use blades primarily but are devastating at hand-to-hand combat. Quinton uses dual pistols, and all three can cast."

"And this Lyrra?" he asked. "What kind of threat is she?"

"Lyrra is a Night Warden, a mage, and a heartless bitch." I narrowed my eyes at him. "Probably not as powerful as you right now, but she fights dirty and isn't afraid to risk her own life if it means taking yours."

"Oh, so she's a typical Night Warden, then," he said with a glance into the park. "So, blast first, and examine what's left afterwards."

"She's one of the best." I felt the tug of Izanami in the back of my skull—a subtle pulling. "Underestimate her and die."

"Did you bring your weapon?"

"Here." I tapped the butt of Fatebringer. "Don't need anything else."

"The DarkSpirit?" He glanced at my holster. "Is it in your bottomless coat?"

"He has it in there," Koda volunteered. "He promised not to use it."

"Can you leave it in the car?" Tristan stared at me and narrowed his eyes. "No—you can't, can you? The bond is too strong now."

"It's under control." I pulled my duster closed and headed into the park. "Let's go."

"Stryder, if you lose it in there…" he began.

"Feel free to ghost me—*after* we stop Lyrra."

THIRTY-TWO

CENTRAL PARK AT night is an ominous open space. Shadow Helm used to occupy the center of the Great Lawn, which was dominated by six softball fields now. When it was standing, the Keep allowed the Night Wardens a base of operations inside the park with an extensive network of tunnels throughout the city.

Until the Purge. The supernatural community felt the Wardens were too much of an obstacle. They joined to combat their common enemy and destroyed Shadow Helm, along with more than half of the Night Wardens, in a bloody year of warfare.

I'd lost many good friends that year. We finally convinced the supernaturals that it was better to live with us than die by our hands, but the damage was done. The decimation of the Night Wardens forced us into the shadows. Soon after, the formation of the NYTF and the Dark Council made them redundant, and they were disbanded except for a small token force.

"I thought the Night Wardens were considered obsolete?" Tristan asked as we approached. "What is this Lyrra doing—planning a coup?"

"The Wardens were shut down after the Purge, but some of us kept patrolling," I said, irked at being called obsolete. I was only a century older than he was, still in my prime. "Lyrra is insane. I guarantee whatever she's planning will shed gallons of blood, and give her what she always wanted—power."

"An army of rummers and ogres will certainly do that," he said as we approached the edge of the lawn. "More importantly, how did she manage to modify the Redrum to make them UV-resistant?"

"She had help." I checked Fatebringer one last time. "This way."

We stood on the center of the field, and I placed my hand on a large stone plaque commemorating the Institution of Night Wardens for their 'tireless service' in keeping the city safe.

"What kind of help?" Tristan stepped back as a large orange circle formed in front of us. "I thought the lower levels were sealed?"

"They were." I looked at the circle in surprise, as a large ramp appeared in the center of the lawn ahead of us. "What the hell is this? What happened to the door?"

The ramp was easily thirty feet across and descended for another forty feet before making a sharp right turn. I could see the dormant runes etched into the stone along the edges. They were designed for enhanced concealment with little to no ambient energy being expended. Lyrra never had the finesse for this kind of rune work.

"Montague, look at these runes." I pointed to the

symbols in the stone. "This is sophisticated work. Too delicate for Lyrra."

"Looks like the work of a Smith." Tristan knelt down and touched the ramp. "This is a recent construction, but it makes sense."

"How does a ramp make sense?" I growled in frustration. "It's supposed to be a small door."

"If I needed to move an army from an underground bunker," he said patiently, "I wouldn't use a door."

"And to infiltrate an underground bunker—does a ramp work?" I snapped back, upset.

"Not if you want to use stealth," he said. "I recall Night Wardens were more the brash and bold type."

I nodded. "Brash and bold—reckless even. Not suicidal."

"Why aren't they greeting us with extreme violence?" He looked down the ramp, standing, and dusting off his pants.

"I hope you're ready." I drew Fatebringer and nodded again. "We just lost the element of surprise."

"The tablet?" Tristan pointed at the plaque. "Was this your 'secret' way in?"

"Was." I looked around. "Only one other person knew about that entrance, and she's gone. It was keyed to our energy signature."

"It would seem your secret is out," he said, forming an orb of flame and releasing it down the ramp. It hovered mid-air near the bottom. "That should give us some warning."

I turned to Koda next to us.

"I'll understand if you want to bail." I looked at the ramp and shook my head. "No way can you secure this ramp alone."

"I'm staying." Her voice cut through the night with an edge. "I'll hold this entrance. Go stop that crazy Night Warden."

She flicked both wrists and the fans materialized in her hands. She sat near the top of the ramp and faced outward to the lawn.

"Remember what I said." I headed down the ramp with Tristan next to me. "You find yourself in over your head, you cut and run to safety."

"Go kick ass, old man." She kept her back to me and raised an arm. "I'll make sure nothing gets in. You make sure nothing gets out."

"Is she a Night Warden?" Tristan glanced up the ramp at Koda. "She seems tense."

"Facing death has a tendency to make most people tense." I walked around his floating orb. At the bottom of the ramp, a large steel door covered in angry runes faced us. I heard the foghorn of destruction and pushed it to the back of my mind.

He narrowed his eyes and shook his head. "The door is set to detonate if tampered with," Tristan said, examining the runes.

"Instantaneous or delayed?"

"Delayed, if I'm reading them correctly," he said after a few seconds. "Looks to be about thirty seconds, give or take."

"Is that expensive suit runed for protection?" I pointed at him. "Or is that just the height of mage fashion on High Street?"

"Runed?" He scoffed. "This is a Zegna Bespoke. I wouldn't allow it to be *runed for protection*. I'm a mage."

I rubbed the material of his sleeve between my fingers and nodded sagely. "That *is* an exceptional suit." I lifted my sleeve to compare. "This is off the rack and runed to protect my ass from everything except a nuclear blast or being stomped on by a dragon."

"Are you sure it *hasn't* been stomped on by a dragon?" He rubbed the material of my duster between his fingers and then rubbed them on the wall next to us. "It's looking a little worse for wear."

"Let's see who looks better in thirty seconds," I said and triggered the runes on the door.

THIRTY-THREE

LYRRA'S MISTAKE WAS adding a delay to the detonation. My mistake was not listening to my own advice and underestimating her. As soon as I stepped close to the door, a large circle appeared beneath me, rooting me in place.

The runes on the door blasted the foghorn of destruction and erupted in orange energy. Tristan looked around the corner and noticed I wasn't moving.

"Are you really planning on testing the limits of Aria's handiwork?"

"I'm stuck." I tried shifting my weight, but the circle was made up of a weave of spells. One made me lighter and the other held me in place. I had no leverage to get myself free.

"Clever—a timed runic stasis," he said and examined the circle. "Whoever set this trap expected proximity to the door. It should release you in about forty-five seconds."

"Glad you can admire the handiwork." I looked at him. "Forty-five seconds is fifteen seconds too long."

"Indeed." He started gesturing. "I can place a shield in front of you, but I have to assume whoever set the trap would factor that in and act accordingly to counter the shield."

"Do it." He nodded, and I gritted my teeth. I was going to have to cast. Aria knew my limitations around casting. The duster operated on passive magic. The reason Tessa wanted it so badly was because of its active properties. "You'd better get back. I need to cast."

"Is that a good idea?" he asked, concerned.

"Can you stop the detonation?"

"Yes, if I had thirty minutes instead of less than twenty seconds."

"You'd better step back, then." He stepped around the corner and activated the shield in front of me. An orange arc of energy formed in front of me. I crouched down, raised the coat to cover my body, and braced against the pain I knew was coming.

I spoke the words of power that activated the coat. The sensation of liquid lava burned through my chest as my muscles seized. The duster went from dark brown leather to black with a metallic sheen. I gritted my teeth against the pain and enclosed myself in the coat.

The foghorn of destruction rose in a crescendo and the door exploded. The blast of energy buffeted me, followed by hundreds of small impacts I could only assume were projectiles of some sort. It was smart, unexpected, and deadly—just like Lyrra.

Several seconds later, the circle underneath me vanished, and I looked around. I stood in a small island of uncharred floor. Small nails were spread out on the floor everywhere.

Tristan walked over as I took a moment to gather myself. I stood with a grunt as he picked up a large handful of the nails with a handkerchief.

"Runed and poisoned." He held it up and turned it. "This Lyrra doesn't want visitors."

He wrapped up a handful of the nails and put the handkerchief in a pocket.

"The spell was a dual cast." I examined the outside of the duster. It reverted to its dark brown leather and I noticed that none of the nails had punctured the material. "Aria's reputation is still intact."

"Like your coat," he said, raising an eyebrow at my duster. "My shield wouldn't have protected you from the nails."

"No, they were designed to cut through magic." I approached the door while looking for a handle. "Casting a shield to deal with the blast would leave you vulnerable to the nail attack, with no time to react."

"They were expecting a mage." He nodded. "But they weren't expecting you."

"Their mistake." I found a panel next to the door. "Think you can bypass this?"

The idea of casting again, even something simple like reversing a lock, made my head throb. The pain was getting worse with each cast. I noticed several of the runes inscribed on the wall were set for timed explosions. It was Lyrra's way of making sure she had an escape route. If those were triggered, we would be out of time.

He walked over to the panel and nodded. "Once I

do this, they *will* know we're here."

"Oh, you mean the explosion wasn't a clue?"

"The explosion was a passive deterrent," he said, forming runes in the air that floated at the panel. "This is an active magical incursion. This means they will know we survived the explosion and send someone or something to investigate."

I heard another distant foghorn.

The door opened, and I felt the three ogres before I saw them. They rounded a corner, jerked their arms, and cracked their necks. One of them bared a hideous smile with yellow teeth. Standing behind and dwarfed by the three monstrosities, stood one of the Twins.

"I'm going to go with: they sent *something*," I said as we entered the large hangar-like space. Vehicles were parked around the edges of the room. Large shelving units created aisles and rows of storage materials. Covered in dust, they appeared untouched since the Purge. The door slammed shut behind us, and I could sense the detonation trap reset itself.

"Three ogres?" he muttered under his breath. "Maybe they *did* expect you."

"Lyrra believes in being thorough." I opened my duster to allow easier access to Fatebringer. "I'm surprised there isn't a pack of rummers as well."

"Hello, Stryder," the Twin said. "I told Lyrra we should have killed you back at that dump you call a bar, but she wants you to join us."

"Join you?"

"She's restoring the Night Wardens, Stryder."

"To what?" I felt my face flush as the anger rose. "We never murdered innocents—or does Lyrra consider the rummers acceptable losses?"

"I told her you wouldn't understand. You lack her vision. Too interested in *justice*, not the law."

"We always stood for justice. We fought for those who couldn't fight for themselves, we were their voice. That's what it meant to be a Night Warden. We had honor."

"That honor was real helpful during the Purge."

I nodded. I wasn't here to have a meeting of the minds. Lyrra had convinced those with her that the only way to regain respect was to rip the power from those she felt had it. They had become the very thing Night Wardens stood against.

In her mind, if that meant sacrificing the homeless or anyone else to achieve her ambition, the ends justified the means.

"I never bothered to learn your names. Which do you prefer? Thing one or Thing two?" I drew Fatebringer. "Either works for me."

"The name is Rina, asshole," she said with a glare. "I'll whisper it in your ear as I cut off pieces of you and feed it to them."

"Rina Asshole, got it—that's pretty exotic." I smiled. "Is that Scandinavian?"

"Are you deliberately trying to piss her off?" Tristan said under his breath. "Because it seems to be working, judging from her expression."

"Yes," I muttered, still holding the smile. "Mages are a touchy bunch. Wouldn't you agree, Mr. Wizard?"

"I'm not a wiz—touché." He nodded and formed two flame orbs.

"I'm going to personally gut you." Rina growled,

unsheathing two blades and held them in a hammer grip.

"Don't dismiss her," I said, stepping to the side. "She prefers her blades, but she's a strong mage."

"Duly noted." He formed another orb and held it in place in front of him. "Are these Redrum ogres?"

"Can't tell yet, but you'll know."

"I'll take the mage," he said, blading his body. "You can have the ogres."

"Don't strain yourself or anything," I said as we walked forward.

"It's not like you can cast," he said. "This makes the most sense."

"I don't want to explain to Rox why you were ghosted. Keep your ass alive."

"I can say the same to you—don't become a ghost."

I shook my head. "It's not 'don't become'—nevermind."

"Crush them." Rina advanced on us. "Leave the old one alive. I'm going to enjoy seeing your intestines all over the floor, Stryder."

The ogres rushed at us—fast.

I greeted Ogre One with two shots in the forehead, dropping him and turning him to dust. I gave silent thanks to Tessa for the negation rounds and dived to the side as Ogre Two tried to introduce my face to his fist.

"She said to crush you, but I may forget myself and accidentally kill you, wizard." Ogre Two said with what I think was a grin. It was too disturbing to look at. More importantly, aside from the unnatural speed, it was forming intelligent, coherent statements. I didn't like what this strain of Redrum was doing. Ogres were creatures whose main purpose was the wholesale and complete destruction of basically—everything. Redrum making them smarter? Terrible idea.

"I'd like to forget you, too." I let my senses expand and realized Ogre Three was trying to flank me. "When did you guys get so smart?"

"Lyrra made us this way," Ogre Two said and lunged as I backpedaled. "We will rule this city by her side."

An orb of flame sizzled by my head as Rina gave me the finger. Tristan closed in on her and she got busy trying to stay alive. I ducked under a swipe and leaped forward into a roll to avoid a foot stomp. I overshot my leap and ended up next to ogre three—who greeted me with a backhand that introduced me to a world of pain as I slid across the floor.

"I said don't kill him!" I heard Rina scream as she released a barrage of daggers at Tristan. "Break him— just don't kill him."

"You heard her, break him," Ogre Two said. "Just leave him breathing."

They rushed forward. For a split second, my brain listed several spells that would neutralize them both in gruesome and messy ways. It took me a moment to realize it wasn't me, but Izanami.

"Don't need the help, thanks."

<I was merely pointing out your options, mage.>

"How are you even speaking to me from inside the coat?"

<We are nearly one. All I require to complete the bond is blood—your blood.>

She whispered the last part like a lover whispered a

name. It felt like a violation. It was wrong and it pissed me off.

"Shut up or I'll melt you down myself."

<And accelerate your death. We are intertwined, mage.>

I raised the duster to absorb another blow. Being hit by a moving bus felt gentler. The coat dissipated most of the blow as the impact sent me sprawling, but my arm felt like jelly.

I took aim and gifted Ogre Two with three rounds, center mass. He looked down at his chest and then up at me. He was about to say something, but the words died on his lips, along with the rest of him as he burst into dust.

"Two shots left," I muttered as Ogre Three ducked behind a row of large metal crates for cover. For a second, my brain couldn't process the image. Ogres never took cover. They rushed headlong to their targets. Through walls if necessary.

<You would never run out of ammunition with me. If you bond with me, you will become the weapon.>

"No, thanks. You creep me the hell out."

I opened Fatebringer and emptied the cylinder, while speed-loading another seven negation rounds. I was about to move into position when I heard the metal scraping. The Ogre had grabbed a container from one of the shelves and launched it in my direction.

The duster could probably withstand the impact, but I wasn't about to find out. I slid forward under the arc of the large metal box and fired twice. Two rounds buried themselves in the ogre's throat. It clutched its neck and tried to speak. All I heard was a rough gargle before it decorated the shelving with more dust.

I wondered why Tristan was holding back from ghosting Rina, when I saw the runes along the floors. Dampeners were etched all over the surface. She had a pendant around her neck. Every time she released an orb, it would pulse a brighter orange. It seemed to counter the effect of the dampeners on her casting.

I took aim at the pendant, adjusted a fraction of an inch to compensate for movement, and fired twice. The first round hit her square in the chest. The second round punched through the muscle of her heart, tearing through it mercilessly. Shock registered on her face as she looked in my direction and grabbed her chest. She was dead before she hit the floor.

I walked over to her body, took her blades, and put them in a pocket. I removed the pendant and tossed it to Tristan. "Next time—you get the ogres."

"She was quite formidable." He examined the pendant and grasped it in one hand while he gestured with the other. The pendant did its pulsing, and he nodded. "This should be adequate."

"I'm glad you approve." I looked down at Rina. "She has a sister who is just dying to meet us."

"You're worse than Simon," he said with a wince. "Two more levels?"

"Yes." I looked around the floor. "I'm surprised Lyrra hasn't unleashed rummers on us."

"I'm certain she will, once we locate her position." He put the pendant on and gestured around it. "It's been my experience that the leaders of these movements prefer to have someone do the fighting for them."

"She'll fight," I said after a pause. "She was the

Night Warden combat instructor. If she isn't here to greet us, something else is going on. Don't let your guard down. Over there."

I pointed at the stairwell that would lead us to the next level below. Down the corridor, I saw a bank of elevators. I wasn't about to put myself in a metal box with no way out so she could just ghost me like a fool. I was crazy, not suicidal.

THIRTY-FOUR

WE REACHED THE second level. I examined the wall and saw more of the detonation runes, when an explosion rocked the floor above us.

"Your partner?" Tristan said, looking up.

"Doubt it." I let my senses expand and felt the presence of something large and disturbing. I didn't sense her particular 'nothingness.' What I did sense gripped me by the gut and squeezed. "Oh, shit, Lyrra, you're one twisted bitch."

"What is it?"

"Koda is fine." I shook off the feeling of dread. "My guess is she took off, which is probably the smartest thing she's done in her life. She won't be coming down here."

"Are you certain?" He narrowed his eyes at me. "What did you sense?"

"Trolls." The silence descended on us like a weight, as we both strained to hear any evidence of the creatures.

"Are you sure?" His face hardened. "I know Night

Wardens have sensory training to read their surroundings, but the range is limited. Can you be mistaken?"

"I hope so." I approached the door to the second level, but kept my distance. I examined the door but detected nothing odd. "Just hasn't happened yet in my lifetime."

"Bloody hell." He looked upstairs with a look of concern. "Ogres on Redrum are difficult enough, but trolls would be almost impossible."

"It has to be a mistake." I kept my voice even as I examined the wall and floor around the door. "There hasn't been a troll in the city since the war."

"Wrong," he said, looking at me. "Simon was chased by one a while back. We barely managed to stop that *one* and we had a soul render."

"The date that flattened Masa, Flat Earth, and a large part of the city…that was a troll?"

"Just one." He nodded, looking around the door.

"I thought that was just you two—well, mostly you."

He glared at me and shook his head. "It was *the troll.*"

"Sorry," I said, raising a hand in surrender. "It had your signature 'obliterate every building in proximity' feel to it."

"We'll have to resort to more conventional methods to attack the weak spots, unless you have a soul render in your bottomless pockets?"

"I forgot to pack my troll-killers." I patted my coat. "Because I usually walk around with rare artifacts of power."

"Like the blade of power you are carrying." He looked at the duster. "Can you use it without succumbing?"

"Not an option," I said, my voice hard. "We discussed this."

"We may be left without the option."

"Do you have a spell that can do the job without sucking us into a void vortex?"

"Their resistance would require me to cast something beyond a void vortex," he replied, and I knew what he was going to say next. "I would have to unleash an entropic dissolution."

"Shit. Hell no." I shook my head. "Let's find Lyrra and end this. Do you sense anything on the door?"

He approached the door, standing next to me. "I don't sense any stasis traps on or around the area. In fact, I don't see any runes on this door at all."

"It's never this easy with her." I grabbed the handle of the door and turned it. It opened onto the second level. This floor, unlike the top level, was bare. About half the size of the first level, it was used as a training area when the Keep was active.

I could still see the faded lines on the floor of the training circles and battle quadrants.

"Training level?" Tristan looked both ways as we stepped in slowly. "No dust on the floor."

"Looks like the floor is being used—but rummers and ogres don't need training."

"How many Night Wardens has Lyrra recruited to her cause?"

"There weren't many of us left to recruit, but if she did a whole 'restore the Night Wardens to glory' campaign, she would convince some of the older members, the rummers and ogres would intimidate the others."

"How many Wardens were left after the Purge?"

"I never took a census, I was blacklisted as a dark mage after Jade," I said. "Shadow Helm was destroyed and these levels were sealed off. We were scattered to the wind, except for a few who remained as symbols of our glorious past—relics to be paraded when it suited the Dark Council or the NYTF."

"I didn't mean to…It would have been good to know if we were facing a hundred Night Wardens or a thousand."

"One hundred or a thousand, the outcome is the same: We don't walk away."

"That's encouraging." He looked behind us.

"Thinking of going back?"

"No, I felt a surge of magic." He frowned at the door. "What's that?"

The door slammed shut behind us and the floor activated. Circles flashed on and off all around us in a random sequence. We stood in a small area by the door, a designated safe zone, which would be safe until a circle formed under our feet and erased us.

"Fuck me." I shook my head and looked around for higher ground. Now I understood why the room was empty. "We need to get off the floor. The room is set to lethal levels."

I heard the sharp intake of breath as the first of the circles formed near us and disappeared.

"*Oblivion circles?*" he exclaimed right before I heard the foghorn of death. Rummers were rushing at us from across the floor.

THIRTY-FIVE

"IS THIS THE welcome you were expecting?"

"How sensitive are you to magical surges?" I said as I reloaded Fatebringer.

"If you're going to ask me if I can feel disturbances in the force, I'll shove you into a circle myself."

"What? No." I pointed at the floor. "The circles are random but they require energy. There's a subtle surge right before each one forms. This is how Night Wardens hone their sensing skills."

"My apologies," he said, raising a hand. "It's clear I've spent too much time around Simon."

"These circles help Night Wardens sense magical fluctuations around them," I said. "The greater the skill, the greater the area of awareness."

"You use lethal oblivion circles," he said, staring at the floor ahead of us. "Bloody hell, you're all daft. It's not surprising there aren't many of you left."

The wave of rummers had reached the middle of the floor. Farther back, I could make out the other Twin.

"The lethal setting is used once the skill is mastered —takes decades." I looked at the approaching rummers. One had stepped into a circle, triggering it, and burst into dust a second later. "Clearly Lyrra intends to end us here."

"I'm curious," he asked with mock seriousness, "what gave it away? The horde of rummers or the oblivion circles getting progressively closer?"

"Don't stand still." I stepped several feet to the side as a circle formed next to me.

He formed several hundred miniature orbs and unleashed them. They ejected small filaments and rested on the ground, connected to each other.

"That should help," he said and gestured. The orbs created a lattice. "I don't have your skill but this is the next best thing."

I nodded. "Clever." I shot two rummers, turning them to dust as they closed in on us. "We need to get to the other side, where the controls for the floor are."

With the pendant around his neck, his casting was at full strength. I could see him getting angrier with each rummer he erased. I would've worried if it didn't bother him.

"These deaths are senseless," he said under his breath. He released several more orbs, blasting the rummers into circles and ghosting them. "Someone capable of this kind of slaughter needs to be eliminated. Lyrra needs to die."

"If the twin upstairs was Rina, this is Willow." I shot three more rummers, followed by two more. I emptied the cylinder and speed loaded another seven. "She's not a blade master, like her sister. This one will cast. Be careful with her misdirection."

<If you used me, these creatures would prove insignificant.>

"Thanks for the tip. You can shut up now."

"I didn't say a word," Tristan answered, confused. "Are you hearing voices?"

"Yes." I dodged away from a rummer's swipe and fired, reducing it to nothing. Another rummer raked the back of my duster, and Tristan blasted through it with a fire orb. "Recent development with the sword."

"May I ask, does the voice sound like Vinnie Jones?"

"The actor?" I stared at him for a second before I leaped forward to avoid another circle. "I think you really need a vacation from your partner. Why would it sound like Vinnie Jones?"

"Never mind." He stepped back and pivoted at the last second to let a rummer lunge past him and into a circle. He looked suddenly behind us. "We have company."

I turned just in time to see the door bulge inward and explode. On the other side of the large hole, a face peeked through, and then the wall began to crumble. The wall collapsed and a large figure stepped through. He was easily eight feet tall and half as wide. I took in the complete image, and it wasn't pretty. Behind the one that broke through the wall, I saw another face, equally ugly.

Tristan gestured and a wall of energy formed, blocking the trolls' advance. "That won't stop them forever," he said as the trolls started pounding on the energy wall. "It also seems they're immune to the circles."

"Trolls." I looked across the room at Willow. "How

the hell did Lyrra get trolls?"

"Irrelevant," Tristan said, moving across the floor faster. "We need to put some distance between them and us."

"Too many rummers ahead, unless you can cast an entropic vortex?"

He gave me a hard stare. "You're asking me to combine the components of two highly unstable and dark spells."

I had several reasons for asking him to cast this spell. I needed to know his current power level after his shift, and his willingness to attempt a dark spell. Everyone had heard about the void vortices he cast in the city, but he wasn't showing any indication of going dark. His reluctance was a good sign. Any mage who was eager to try dark spells was a threat—to themselves and the city. I should know.

I would hate to have to ghost him if he lost it and went dark. Rox would fry my ass several times over if it came to that. I'd rather face the angry trolls intent on stomping us than an angry Rox.

"Not dark—gray." I gave him a shrug. "If you're too scared to do it, I guess I can cast it. I w that with your recent power shift, you would be able to handle this. No worries. I'll be out of it for a while afterwards. Can you handle the trolls on your own?"

"I'll do it." He glared at me. "Only because you're too old and infirm to handle the rigors of the casting. It's not like the Golden Circle is going to tack more death to my sentence."

"And the two trolls." I added, pointing behind us.

"And the two trolls—yes." He gestured and began

blending the runes.

"For someone who isn't a dark mage, you know the obscure runes well." I glanced over as a rummer leaped at him. I fired, dusting him mid-air.

"I study *all* the runes. It's why I'm a mage and not a wizard," he said. "If I get this wrong, we won't be around to discuss the error. I don't even know if it will work."

"You're basically creating a large, free-form, negation round in vortex form." I ghosted another rummer that approached, and jumped to the side to avoid a circle. "It'll work."

"Oh, that's all, is it?" he said as he gestured, and the area around him grew dark. "I'm doing this against my better judgment."

"I understand." Mages and their egos. We were a sorry lot when pushed. "Let me get clear. I'll stop Willow and explain the error of her ways—violently."

I ran forward, avoiding circles as they appeared before me. I had to stop a few times and backtrack as they formed in clusters too large to jump over.

I saw Willow casting in the distance. She stood in the center of a protective circle. Nothing I fired would reach her through that shield. I needed her outside of it and irrational. I slowed my pace, emptied Fatebringer, and speed loaded more negation rounds.

I had a speed loader with entropy rounds, but I was saving those for Lyrra. I knew they were banned, but she deserved no less than to have her body torn and ripped apart. I was thoughtful that way.

As I closed the distance, Willow noticed me and sent a flame orb my way. I raised my duster to take the brunt of the impact. The orb crashed into my side, sending flames everywhere.

"Stryder, why don't you die already?" she said and formed another orb. "No one wants you around—you're a relic."

I needed to time it perfectly. She was dangerous with her flame orbs. Another rummer lunged at me. I kicked it into a circle, turning it to dust. I stood my ground. I would have to drive her into a rage, angry enough to come at me herself. I knew just the button to push, but first the rummers had to be stopped.

"Anytime you want to let that go would be good." I glanced back at Tristan. He held a large mass of dark energy in front of him.

"Would you like to hold this?" I could tell it was difficult to maintain. "It's not like it's unstable or can erase us if I do this wrong."

I sensed a large group of rummers advancing on his position. "You have incoming." I kept my eyes on Willow. "Unleash that thing and get clear."

I felt the surge of energy as he completed the casting. The mass of energy shot forward and enveloped a rummer. It morphed into a small tornado and began drawing the rummers into it and disintegrating them.

"I keyed it to the Redrum so we should be safe, but I wouldn't get too close. It's volatile and unpredictable."

"You're not half bad as a mage." I nodded in grudging admiration.

"I have my moments," he said, dusting off his jacket. "It won't work against the trolls, though. Their resistance is too high, and I won't risk a stronger vortex."

"How long will it last?"

"Not long, but it should remove most of the rummers."

The rummers were being pulled from every direction into the vortex. Keying it to the Redrum meant they didn't stand a chance against the force of the spell. I glanced at Tristan. In a few decades, he was going to be a formidable mage.

The floor shuddered as the trolls roared. The wall holding them back began to collapse, and Willow laughed.

"I don't need to do anything." She pointed behind us. "Those two will rip you apart."

Tristan faced the trolls. "I'll slow them down. You stop her and get this floor shut down." He gestured as he closed the distance on the trolls.

"Rina went quick." I stepped to the side to avoid a circle forming under me. "I made sure she didn't feel pain. It wasn't what she deserved, but it was right."

"Fuck you, Stryder," she hissed, taking a step toward me. "No way could you take down my sister."

I removed Rina's blades from my pocket and tossed them on the floor in front of her as I stepped back, careful not to step in a circle.

"Those look familiar?" I asked, knowing what the response would be. "She wasn't as skilled as she thought. Maybe she missed some of the training?"

Her face transformed into a mask of fury as she bent down to pick up the blades. They burst into flame as she channeled magic through them. I stepped back several more feet.

"I'm going to kill you myself, old man." She leaped at me, jumping out of the protective circle—exactly as I planned.

My duster was strong and I had confidence in Aria and her word-weaving spells, but Willow's blades were covered in some nasty runes and looked dangerous. I didn't want to take the chance of being cut by them.

Most of the Night Wardens believed I couldn't cast. I had spread the rumor of an erasure early on as the consequence of my casting the dark spell. Only a few people knew the truth of my condition.

Willow approached, expecting me to use Fatebringer. I didn't disappoint her. I raised my gun and fired at her three times. She deflected the rounds with her sister's blades.

"At least you use them better than your sister." I needed her closer and irrational. I holstered Fatebringer. "She died with a look of surprise on her face."

She screamed at me and attacked. Swinging wildly, she slashed at my face. I slid to the side, gestured, and held my breath against the stab of pain in the back of my neck. She slashed again. I ducked under her attack as I placed a hand on her side, pushing her back and releasing the spell into her body.

I stumbled back and fell on my side, narrowly missing a circle as she kicked at my head. I raised my arms in a cross-block and deflected most of the impact. She stabbed down as I rolled to the side, dodging the flaming blade.

My vision tunneled in as I fought to maintain consciousness. I staggered to my feet as she laughed.

"Why don't you just surrender, old man?" She feinted with a blade, and I stepped back out of range. "I'll finish you quick, you bastard."

"That's really considerate of you." I got my breathing under control and spat blood to the side. "But you're already dead…your brain just hasn't gotten the memo."

"I'm dead?" she scoffed. "I'm not the one spitting up blood."

"The first lesson you learn as a Night Warden— stack the odds in your favor." I moved back. "Don't fight fair, because fair doesn't exist. Misdirect and attack from strength when you appear weak."

"Time to die." She took a step forward, dropped one of the blades, and clutched her side. "What did you do?"

"I killed you."

She took another step and fell to her knees, dropping the other blade. She formed an orb of flame as I shook my head. She was about to unleash it when the orb sputtered and disappeared.

I saw real fear on her face then, and for a split second, through the haze of pain threatening to split my head in half, I almost felt sorry for her.

"What did you hit me with?" The fear was evident now as the pain increased and seized her side. "You can cast—they told me you couldn't cast."

"A devourer spell." I drew Fatebringer. "You're looking at ten minutes of pure agony. It'll eat your insides and leave your nerves intact. You'll feel everything right up until the moment you're ghosted."

"Stryder, no," she gasped through the pain that

racked her body. Her eyes were wide with fear. "Finish it. I don't—I don't want to suffer. Not like this."

I fired Fatebringer once and saved her the pain. I limped over to the control room in the back. The runic controls were on the far side. I placed my hand on them and disabled the training circles, as the sound of a thunderclap filled the level.

THIRTY-SIX

I LOOKED ACROSS the floor to see the trolls destroy the energy wall and step farther into the room.

"You right bastard. Come on, then." I heard the voice but couldn't believe it. It was Frank. He was facing one of the trolls when a bolt of electricity exploded in the room, charring one of the trolls and catapulting the other across the floor.

I saw Tristan lean against the wall and pat the sweat from his forehead with a handkerchief. I walked by the unconscious troll that had flown across the floor. Smoke wafted up from his body as I stared at the small lizard. Next to him stood Koda, looking battered but mostly intact.

"What the hell are you doing down here?" I said to them. "You"—I pointed at Koda—"I told you to cut and run if things got bad. And you, *lizard*, are supposed to be at The Dive. Where's Cole?"

Frank stepped up close, and I could feel the electrical charge in the air around him. "I can see you've been getting your ass kicked, so I'm going to disregard the lizard comment." He pointed one small leg at me and spat to the side.

"How did you get down here?"

A small ball of electricity raced across the floor and exploded against the far wall. "I think the words you're looking for are: 'thank you for saving my ass from two large scary trolls that were going to shred me and my mage friend', oh great powerful *dragon*."

"How did you even get past the doors?" I looked at Koda. "Is this your idea of getting away?"

"You told me to get to safety," she said, sticking out her chin and squaring off. "They appeared right outside the entrance you told me to guard and could see through my camouflage."

"Does this look remotely safe to you?" I threw up my hands. "I told you to get safe—*away* from here. Not further into the danger."

"That was probably my fault, Grey," Frank said and looked back at the destruction behind us. "She must have seen me run in. Sassy-pants is a great lockpick. She got past all the defenses, no problem."

"I followed him and they followed me," Koda said. "I didn't have a choice. Besides, you said run *to* safety." She looked around at the devastation. "Next to you two is the safest place down here."

"She does have a point," Tristan said.

"Shut it, Montague." I pinched the bridge of my nose to stave off the impending migraine. "No way are they coming downstairs. I haven't even seen Quinton, and I can guarantee he won't be as easy as the Twins."

"Montague?" said Frank. "As in Poindexter Montague?"

"He's my uncle," Tristan said, looking warily at Frank. "But no one calls him that. At least no one living. How do you know him?"

"Ha! Old Stone Fist?" Frank responded, looking around. "Now, that's a mage you want on your side in a battle—no offense meant. He would have smeared those trolls without breaking a sweat."

"None taken, I think," Tristan said. "You know my Uncle Dex? He never mentioned a liz—I mean, dragon —of your scale."

Frank shook his body, sending bolts of electricity in every direction. "I wasn't always in this body," he said with another shake. "It's complicated. Anyway, is Dex with you?"

I stared at Frank. "No, *Dex* isn't with us," I snapped. "Maybe when we're done here, you can have Tristan put you in touch. While you're at it, don't you have some other long lost relatives or friends you need to locate?"

"Someone hasn't had their coffee today." Frank stepped around to Koda's side and stood behind her legs. "Don't be so touchy. I was just asking. If Dex isn't here" —he looked Tristan up and down—"I guess his nephew will have to do. Are you any good?"

"I can hold my own."

"See? There." Frank pointed at Tristan. "It's good to have a Montague on your side in a fight. Even if they are a bit scrawny and have no clue how to dress for a proper battle. Where were you headed when Grey called you—a funeral?"

"I was—" Tristan started.

"Don't bother," I said. "You two get topside, now.

Tristan and I can handle things from here."

"Handle things?" Koda crossed her arms over her chest and glared at me. "Both of you look like you can barely stand—you especially."

"I'm fine, we're fine," I growled. "This is too dangerous. I don't want you getting in over your head."

"We could use the help," Tristan said. "You look like bloody hell, and I feel the way you look."

"Thanks for the vote of confidence," I grumbled as I made my way across the floor. "How soon before the trolls come to, Frank?"

"Not in this lifetime," he said and kept walking. "What? Did you think they were going to have a chat with you? Trolls only exist to destroy and kill. Thought you knew that."

I stared at him with a newfound respect and just the smallest amount of fear.

"What did you do?"

"I fried their tiny little brains." He poked the troll that lay face down in the middle of the floor, not unconscious—dead. The other one was a charred mess, but I could've sworn this one was still alive when it landed.

"You what?" I said, still shocked that he could take down two trolls alone.

"Magic resistance is off-the-charts with these things, so I used straight electrical energy." He pointed at his eyes and made an explosion sound. "Through the eyes and into the brain...poof. No more angry troll. Worse than a soul render."

"You're one scary dragon." I headed to the stairwell leading down.

"Now you're finally starting to understand." He stood on his hind legs and balanced with his tail. "Lockpick," —he reached for Koda—"do me a favor and help me with the stairs?"

THIRTY-SEVEN

WE REACHED THE lower level.

The wall holding the door was covered in runes. I kept my distance and made sure no one approached that side of the level.

Tristan narrowed his eyes as he examined the door.

"Several layers of traps." He shook his head. "Stasis, disintegrating, and all-around nastiness. Bollocks, there's no way around that door."

I looked around the corridor. All of the surfaces were smooth stone. The door was the only break in the wall, and if I remembered correctly, it was six inches thick.

In addition to the runes, the door itself was made of a tungsten-titanium tempered alloy, treated to be magically resistant *before* the runes were etched into it.

"We could detonate a nuclear weapon on top of that door. There's a good chance it'll be the only thing standing after the explosion," I said, reluctant to consider the other possibility.

"There's a way." Koda looked at me, and I shook my

head.

"No way," I said. "We don't know what kind of traps are on that thing besides the nastiness we can see. There could be plenty we don't see."

"What did this level contain?" Tristan asked, pulling out the plans. He smoothed them on the floor and pointed to the area where we stood. "This level is self-contained."

"This was the armory and artifact storehouse," I said, still giving Koda the stink-eye. "Inner Armory and Outer Armory—Rare weapons, weapons of unknown origin, and artifacts we studied were kept on this level. There was also a twenty-four-hour Warden Guard, two stationed outside the door and two inside."

"That would explain the runes and the door." He rubbed his chin. "Are the weapons and artifacts still contained here?"

"No, after the Purge and before the destruction of Shadow Helm, the contents of this level were sent to the Cloisters for safekeeping in their archive."

The magic on this level gave off a high-pitched tone. It was a sound I associated with refined, elevated, and dangerous magic. The ambient magic in The Cloisters gave off a similar tone.

Tristan checked the plans several times. "I can't see a way to get in, at least not from these," he said with a sigh. "I'm open to suggestions. Any spell I can think of would just bounce off that door. What is this *way* you were mentioning?"

"I can get past this door," Koda stated with certainty. "I can see how the runes interlock. I know how to get around them."

"That's all well and good," Tristan said. "Even I can see how they're joined. The problem is setting off the traps that will make quick work of you."

"She's a cipher," I answered. "The door won't see her."

"Ciphers don't exist, Stryder." He turned and looked at Koda. "Everything has to have an energy signature…"

The stunned look on his face was priceless. He narrowed his eyes at her and nodded.

"I didn't believe it at first, either."

"The energy she exhibits is from her weapons," he said in analytical mode. "She, however, is a void—no energy signature whatsoever. How is this possible?"

"Good genes." Koda flicked her wrists, materializing her fans. "Stryder, let me do what I do best."

"How about I unleash a bolt at the door?" Frank said with a twitch of his tail. "I can pack quite a blast of energy if I unleash it all."

"And fry us all in the process." I shook my head. "Thanks, Frank, but I'm not in the mood to be barbecued today."

"I'll be careful, Stryder," Koda said, handing me her fans. "Just in case the door picks them up—that would be bad."

"You feel anything go sideways, you get out before it's too late, understand?"

She nodded. "I may need some room, though." She motioned us back. "Can you guys go over there?"

The fans felt heavy in my hand. If she died, it would be because I allowed it. We backed up to the stairwell just to be safe. She approached the door and I winced,

expecting her to be ghosted right there and then. She
sat in front of the door and closed her eyes, taking a
deep breath. I put the fans in my pocket.

That's when I heard the roar. I looked down at
Frank.

"Fried their tiny little brains?" I looked up the stairs
and then at Tristan, who nodded at me. "That doesn't
sound very fried to me."

"Maybe the second one didn't get a big enough jolt?"

"Frank, you stay with Koda," I said, pointing at her.
"You fry anything that comes down these stairs that
isn't us. We're going to check out the troll whose brain
you supposedly fried."

I saw Frank go stand behind Koda. He squared off,
waved his tail, and faced the stairwell. He was eight
inches of barely-contained menace. I nodded to him as
Tristan and I climbed the stairs.

"Have you ever faced a troll?" Tristan asked as we
reached the second level door. "One that wasn't fried, I
mean."

"Ogres and Redrum ogres, yes." I opened the door a
crack. "Trolls—haven't had the pleasure, no."

"It stands to reason that this is a Redrum troll," he
said and gestured. I felt the power surge wash over me.

"What are you doing?" I asked, wary. "This isn't a
dragon, it's a troll. That spell is worse than the entropic
vortex."

"It's not dark, even if it feels that way." He grabbed
the pendant around his neck with his opposite hand.
"This will remove most of the troll's magic resistance,
but I'll need to use this as a power source. I hope
you're packing some serious firepower in that thing. My

casting will be limited after this spell."

"We still have to face Quinton and Lyrra." I checked Fatebringer to make sure I had enough negation rounds in the cylinder.

"We won't be facing anyone if an angry troll rips us to bits."

"I'm running low on ammo, thanks to the rummers."

"I suggest you make every shot count."

"Will do." I stepped back and raised Fatebringer. "Hit him with your spell. I'll put him down."

Tristan pulled open the door and unleashed a barrage of orbs as he ran into the room. The troll turned at the sound of the door. The orbs crashed into its chest with little kinetic force. I followed as the troll raced at us. I slid to the side and fired as the troll cratered the floor with a fist where I'd been standing a second earlier.

It rushed at me, and I fired again. I leaped to the side, narrowly avoiding a kick designed to break me.

"Your stupid weapons have no effect on me, wizard —just like his magic is useless," the troll said and attempted to close the distance. "I'm going to break you."

"Are you sure you lowered its defenses?" I asked as I twisted around a fist the size of my head. "He still seems pretty resistant."

"There might be a delay." He reached into his pocket and pulled out another handkerchief. "This should speed things along."

"What? You're going to wipe away its sweat?"

He ignored me as I ducked under a haymaker and

right into a knee strike. I managed to pull the duster in front my body, which took the brunt of the impact. I landed across the floor with the wind knocked out of me. I felt the tremor of the troll approaching and tried to get up. Spots danced before my eyes, and I slipped to one knee as the troll screamed.

He turned and faced Tristan, now the greater threat. I saw Tristan gesture as he threw something at the troll. The troll clutched at his eyes with a bellow that made me wince.

Nails were embedded in each of its eyes as it raced at Tristan. "Now, Stryder!" he yelled.

I got on both knees, steadied my arm, and fired, emptying the cylinder. The troll burst into flame as runes floated around its body. I looked at Fatebringer, perplexed. The next second, I was being dragged into the stairwell. Tristan slammed the door as the troll exploded. Nails buried themselves in the door and walls.

"I thought you couldn't cast?"

"The dampeners in this place limit my ability, they don't strip it." He started walking downstairs. "Let's see if your partner has made any progress."

I opened the door to the second level slightly. Troll parts littered the floor. I ripped off the sleeve from one of the troll arms and grabbed a bunch of the nails that peppered the wall and door. I wrapped them tightly and put them in a pocket.

"Stryder, get down here!" I heard the panic in Frank's voice and rushed downstairs. "I don't know what happened. One moment she's fine, the next she's gone."

Koda's prone body greeted me as I reached the third level.

THIRTY-EIGHT

"DID SHE SAY anything?" I gently turned Koda over. "What happened?"

"She unlocked the door, and then said something about setting off a trigger." Frank flicked his tail from side to side. "She sounded scared—really scared. Then she froze up and fell on her face. Is she still, you know, breathing?"

Tristan crouched next to her body. "I'm not a medic, but I know some field medicine."

I moved back and let him examine her. Her breathing was shallow but steady.

"Do what you can to get her stable." I scooped up Frank and stepped back. "It's too dangerous here for her. I need you to get her out."

"What do you mean 'get her out'?"" Frank stared at me and twitched his tail. "We're three levels down in this place."

"Frank," I said, "how long have we known each other?"

"Too damn long," he growled.

"Then you know better than to try and bullshit me."

"You don't know what you're asking. The trip alone could kill her."

"If she stays here, it's a guarantee." I looked over to where Koda lay. "Once Lyrra finds out she's a cipher, she'll ghost her."

"What about you?" he asked. "You plan on taking psycho-bitch Lyrra, Quinton, and whatever assorted insanity she has in there on your own with the *GQ* mage?"

"I still have a few cards to play," I said. "He's not half-bad. Just doesn't know how to dress for battle."

"Maybe he thinks it's tea time?" Frank said. "Brits always think it's tea time."

"You do realize I can hear you?" Tristan said and walked over. "I did the best I could. She's stable, but because of her unique condition, I can't assess what runic damage she sustained. I would strongly urge she be taken to Haven."

"You heard the man." I walked over to where Koda lay and placed Frank next to her. "Get her to Rox. She'll know what to do."

"Grey," Frank said, staring up at me, "this card you have to play—is it sword shaped?"

"No," I lied. "I can still cast."

"Now who's trying to bullshit who?" Frank said and looked at Tristan. "You erase psycho-bitch and her pet ogre. Put them down like a pair of rabid dogs."

"Understood," Tristan said, his voice grim.

"One more thing, Montague." Frank stood on his hind legs and leaned forward. "You see Grey lose his shit and go psycho, you put him down too."

Tristan didn't answer, but he stepped back with a nod. I made a fist and extended it to Frank—who fist-bumped me back.

"Get her safe. Tell Rox about her being a cipher, she'll know what to do."

"You ghost these fuckers and get your ass to The Dive, Grey, or I swear I'll come kill you myself," Frank said and twitched his tail. "Now move the hell back, both of you, so I can do this."

I stepped back to the stairwell and was joined a second later by Tristan. Frank spread out his legs and muttered some words under his breath. I saw a ring of energy form around him and Koda.

Electrical energy crackled and arced off his body. I felt the waves of heat fill the space. I heard Frank yell something unintelligible, and a lightning bolt struck them both. The thunderclap that followed was deafening, followed by the sweet pungent smell of ozone.

They were gone.

"That is one scary dragon," Tristan examined the door. "She disabled all of the traps, and the door is unlocked."

"Only one thing left to do." I emptied the cylinder in Fatebringer and replaced the negation rounds with a speed loader. I was down to two loaders of negation and one of entropy. After that I would have to throw Fatebringer at someone.

"Stryder..." He rested a hand on my shoulder. "Are you planning on using the sword?"

"I plan on walking away from this." I turned to face him. "What about you? You plan to die here? You going to let her ghost you and continue killing innocent people, just so she can fulfill some twisted vision of the Night Wardens?"

"If the sword turns you—"

"I told you, if I go 'full dark mage, take-over-the-world-mental,' you better make sure you put me down," I said and took a deep breath. "Trust me, I'd do the same for you."

I pushed open the door and the level exploded.

THIRTY-NINE

"STILL ALIVE?" I heard Quinton's voice. "Good. I was hoping you weren't going to make this easy." He was on the other side of the floor, standing in front of the door that led to the inner armory.

I looked at the debris I lay in. Half the wall was missing. The door, however, was intact.

"Tristan?" I called out looking around for him. I saw his body slumped against the wall. For a split-second, I thought I was going to have a violent conversation with Rox about his demise. He coughed and got to his feet, using the wall as support. I have to admit, I breathed easier when I saw him move. He didn't look happy about the tears in his suit, which brought a tight smile to my lips.

"Bollocks." He looked down at his ruined jacket. "It's completely ruined."

"How's the Zegna Bespoke holding up?"

"It isn't," he said. "Between the rummers and now *this*, it's ruined." He took off the jacket and tossed it to one side.

"I'll get you a duster and then you can look like that awesome wizard in Chicago—what's his name?" I asked, snapping my fingers. "Larry? Barry? Anyway, the one with a beast of a dog with a cute name. He's just like you, goes around destroying the city. Must be a wizard thing."

He glared at me. "I already have a beast," he said, upset. "He and his creature are a handful, thank you very much—and don't call me a wizard."

We stood in the outer armory. The floor was roughly the same size as the training level above us. Along the walls, I saw rows of triple bunk beds with red runes inscribed along their sides. Each bed held a body with an IV bag attached. They all appeared to be in stasis. I counted several hundred beds easily.

"Looks like we found where the rummers are being made." I drew Fatebringer and motioned to the beds. Tristan looked at the setup and clenched his fists.

"Bloody hell," he said. "They're all homeless people."

I nodded and looked across at Quinton, who was laughing.

"You've come to save the trash, Dragonfly?" He drew his guns. I could see the runes come to life from where I stood. "I told Lyrra you'd never come to our side. Too caught up in standing for the forgotten."

"Guns and casting," I said under my breath. "Don't get hit by those bullets. His guns are runed. The rounds will erase both you and your magic."

"Erasure rounds?"

"More like eraser rounds, but yes, nasty." I kept an eye on the rummer beds as I angled for cover. "He calls them magekillers. This would be a good time to cast a shield, if you can."

Quinton wore black combat armor with thigh holsters to hold his cannons. Subtlety was never his strong point. He counted on surprise and intimidation, which usually worked, unless his target didn't care and was ready for his attacks. If that was the case, he was just a large target.

I fired Fatebringer and missed.

I leaped for cover behind one of the medicine cases and examined Fatebringer. His handcannon punched a hole in the wall next to me.

"What's the matter?" he yelled. "Did the famous Dragonfly miss? I should've ghosted you years ago, after you were blacklisted."

I couldn't comprehend how I missed. My gun was in perfect working order, which meant he was using some kind of distortion field to deflect my rounds.

Tristan gestured and threw up a shield. I could see it was a struggle for him to cast. Quinton fired and blew several holes in the shield as Tristan rolled forward. He ended up a few feet away, behind a large storage container.

"I'm open to suggestions. My casting is being affected by dampeners." He wiped the sweat from his forehead as I slid over Fatebringer.

"You want me to shoot him?" He held up the gun and looked at me with an 'are you serious?' look. "Didn't you just miss?"

"No, can you make out the runes?"

He narrowed his eyes and examined Fatebringer. "Yes, this is some intricate rune work."

"Do you see it?" I asked. "The unraveling?"

He shook his head at first and then looked closer. After a few seconds, he nodded and slid Fatebringer back. "I see it, but I can't cast this," he said, looking at me. "This requires a dark mage."

"I know." I sighed and braced myself. "It's an obscure dark spell. I need you to boost my spell when I target his guns."

"Can you do it?" he asked, concerned. "You're looking a little worn."

"Don't see much of a choice," I said and began the gestures. The pain was immediate. An icepick of black agony shoved itself into the side of my head and twisted. I bit down on my tongue until I tasted blood to keep from crying out. The pain blinded me for a few seconds, but I continued the casting. "When I release the orb, you hit it with the unraveling—I'll do the rest."

My vision returned, and I saw the hazy black orb forming in my hand. This time I was causing the foghorn of death. If I did this right, the orb would undo not just Quinton's guns, but Quinton himself. I may have forgotten to explain that part of the spell to Tristan.

I whispered a word of power over the orb and let it go. It hovered in front of me for a few seconds. I felt the boost of runic energy from Tristan and whispered the instruction as the orb sped away, aimed at Quinton.

"What is this pitiful spell?" He fired at the orb, which split in two. The rounds passed through the orbs, leaving them untouched. They cut through the distortion field and latched onto his handcannons, staying there despite his efforts to shake them off.

They moved fast.

In seconds, both guns were in pieces on the floor. I stepped away from the medicine case. "The original name of the spell has been lost to time," I said, closing the distance with Tristan next to me. "I can tell you what it's called now."

"Fuck you, Stryder." He tried shaking his hands but the orbs had transferred from the handcannons to his hands. "I don't need guns to take care of you or your wizard." He tried to gesture and discovered he had lost all motor skill ability. The consistency of the spell was similar to sticking your hands into a vat of honey.

"A creeper," Tristan said with an edge. "I saw this during the war. I thought this spell was banned and then lost."

"It was banned after they created this variation." I gestured again and fell to one knee. Gasping, I stood shakily. "Not lost."

Quinton scoffed as he kept trying to shake the orbs off. "You can't even cast without falling over. Lyrra is going to ghost you before you can blink—old man."

"That may be true, but you won't be here to see it." I uttered a word of power and the creeper went from a spell designed to destroy inorganic material, perfect for disarming your enemies, to destroying organic material, perfect for disarming your enemies—literally.

The screams didn't start right away. It took a few seconds before Quinton realized what was happening.

"Can you stop it?" Tristan asked. "Once that spell gets started, it's almost impossible to stop."

"It's keyed to the unraveling runes from his guns," I said as Quinton began to scream. "Night Warden weapons are tied to their wielders' runic signature."

"Once the runic signature is gone, it will dissipate and become inert," he said. "Simple and lethal."

The creeper had disintegrated Quinton's arms, leaving nothing in its wake. It consumed everything— clothes, skin, muscles, bone, and blood. Everything would be destroyed and converted to fuel the spell until it ran its course.

"Kill me, you bastard," Quinton pleaded through tears. "I hope Lyrra rips you apart. Please—please...it hurts."

I drew Fatebringer and crouched down next to Quinton.

"How many of people in those beds begged for their lives before you forced Redrum into them?" I pointed to the bunk beds as the rage rose inside of me. "How many?"

"It wasn't me—it was all Lyrra." He writhed on the floor and ground his teeth. "I was just following orders. She would've killed me if I didn't do it. She's lost her mind."

I looked at the door to the inner armory. I was certain she was in there waiting for me.

"You should've picked an honorable death, Q." I aimed Fatebringer. "Now I have to put you down like a wounded animal."

"Do it, Stryder."

I pulled the trigger.

The creeper continued to erase all trace of Quinton.

I turned to face Tristan. "I need you to do me a favor."

He looked at me and raised an eyebrow. "We still

have to face Lyrra," he said, giving what was left of Quinton's body a wide berth. "Then we can discuss favors. You can start with my new Zegna."

"I need you to get upstairs and call Rox, the NYTF and the Dark Council." I looked at the rummers in the beds. "This place needs to be sealed—permanently this time. Have them set up a cordon. We can't let these rummers get out."

"That would be a catastrophe." He looked at the beds. "Do you have an exit plan?"

"I'm a dying dark mage, wizard." He winced, and I smiled. "There's no place for me up there. The Night Wardens are finished. I'm just writing the final chapter. *This* is my exit plan."

"What about Koda and your friends?" he asked. "What do I tell them?"

"Tell them the truth." I reached in my duster and pulled out Dark Spirit. "I went out on my terms, doing what was right."

"It was an honor fighting alongside you," he said, extending a hand. I took it and nodded.

"You'll be an excellent mage in a few hundred years." I placed the sword on the table and drew Fatebringer. I emptied the cylinder and speed loaded the entropy rounds. "Keep practicing, and don't go dark."

"I noticed the runes on the levels," he said. "You were never planning on coming back, were you?"

"Like I said, you'll be fairly decent in a few hundred years." I holstered Fatebringer, grabbed the sword, and drew the blade.

"Goodbye, Night Warden Stryder."

"Take care of Rox."

He nodded and took off at a run.

"This is going to be the shortest-lived host you've ever had." I ran the edge of the blade across my forearm and power exploded into my body.

Images raced across my vision. The power burned through me, and I had to grip the table to remain upright. The wound on my arm sealed almost immediately. I felt my magic interlace with the sword, solidifying the bond between us.

<Yes, Mage, finally.>

"Don't get excited. We still have to face one of the strongest Night Wardens I've known, and she's batshit crazy."

<You are still in a weakened state. The best course of action is to retreat until you recover your strength.>

I looked around and shook my head. "I'm afraid that's not an option," I said with a dark laugh. "I'm going to need you to mask your presence until I draw you again. Can you do that?"

<Of course.>

I sheathed the sword, placed it in my duster again, and drew Fatebringer. I pressed my hand against the panel next to the door. The locking mechanism slid back, and the door sighed open.

"Time to die."

FORTY

THE INNER ARMORY was half the size of the outer
armory. The walls were thicker and the runes inscribed
on them more potent. There was no ambient magic,
and silence greeted me as I stepped all the way inside.
Shelves and tables gave it a workshop feel. In the back
of the room was the vault, where the most dangerous
artifacts were stored.

The vault door was ajar, letting me see that the vault
itself was empty. The runes in the vault pulsed with
power, and I noticed a large active circle on the floor. It
seemed out of place, considering artifacts were no
longer being kept here.

I let my senses expand and felt—nothing. No, not
nothing. Someone was masking their runic signature. I
crouched and pulled up my duster in time to deflect a
dark orb aimed at my head. It bounced off the coat
and hit the wall, dissolving the area it hit.

"You know you can't hide, Lyrra," I said, keeping my
coat close to my body. "Why don't you come out so we
can kill each other properly?"

"You should've joined me, Grey," she said. Her voice echoed off the walls, making it hard to pinpoint where she was. "You still can. Together we can restore the Wardens to their glory."

"The Wardens are finished, Lyrra."

"No!"

Another orb of black energy raced at me. I slid to the side as it went past. I dropped to the ground and rolled as it came from behind and burst where I stood.

She materialized then. She was as beautiful as I remembered. Black hair cascaded down her back. Her bronze skin shone in the light as she took a defensive stance. She wore Night Warden leathers—runed to enhance her speed, reflexes, and strength.

This was *not* going to be pleasant.

One glance into her eyes and I knew she had stepped over the edge. "What was the plan?" I asked. "Detonate the upper levels and release the rummers into the city?"

"How did it feel when Jade died in your helpless arms?"

I crushed the anger and rage before it had a chance to rear its head. She wanted me emotional, reacting to her words. I raised Fatebringer and fired—faster than I had ever moved before. She was faster.

An orb crashed into my chest and sent me sprawling. I recovered fast and got to my knees. I needed a different approach.

"It hurt," I said, after a pause. "When I lost Jade, my world ended. Everything that mattered died with her."

"It was your fault, Grey." She formed a black orb and let it dance on her fingers before reabsorbing it.

"You wanted power. It didn't matter what it cost."

"I know—I didn't realize the price would be so high."

"You can join me now," she said softly. "We can fix it. I can stop the poison in your body."

"Do you think I still can?" I stood slowly. "I mean, so much has happened. So much death."

"Only through death do we really appreciate life." She pointed toward the rummers. "Look at them. I gave their life purpose again. They were living on the streets—like trash! Now...now they're mine. My army."

"Now you have an army." I glanced in the direction she pointed. "What will you do with them?"

"We will take this city, Grey," she said. "Take it back from those who wanted to crush us. I—we—will restore the Night Wardens. Do you see it?"

"I see it." I kept my voice even. I needed to get close enough to end her. I took several steps forward, and she jerked her head at me. "We can do this, just you and me."

"Liar." she formed a handful of black and red orbs. Runes danced around them, and I had the feeling that they weren't going to bounce off my duster. "You have power. Real *power* within you. You want to take my army—you want to kill me!"

So much for the sword hiding its presence. I raised Fatebringer, and one of the orbs left her hand and sliced through the barrel. I threw the half I held at her and unsheathed the sword. Black tendrils enveloped me as the sword absorbed the light around it.

"You've killed innocent people—for what?" I kept my eyes on the orbs in her hand and held the sword in front of my body. "This has to end, Lyrra."

"It will," she said. "Right after I kill you."

The orbs flew off her hand and came at me. She gestured and materialized a sword in her hand. I dodged most of the orbs by leaping to the side. Two of them punched right through the duster.

She closed the distance and slashed at me. I parried her thrust and stepped into her with my shoulder in an effort to throw her off balance. She pivoted around my shoulder charge and buried an elbow in the side of my neck.

Pain gripped me as I staggered back and I almost dropped the sword.

<You are fighting the bond. You cannot wage this battle on two fronts. Surrender to the bond or die—your choice.>

"You can't face me, Grey," she said as she circled. "I beat them all. Everyone who called me insane is dead or a rummer now. Even your old patrol mates."

She had killed them all. The Night Wardens I'd known knew were mindless creatures now, lying helplessly in those bunks. I let the rage go and the bond surged in me.

She formed more orbs, but they moved in slow motion as they raced at me. I dodged them as I ran at her. I thrust forward and she parried, turning and swinging to cut my legs. I leaped over her slice, gestured, and blasted her with an orb.

"You can cast?" she said as the orb lifted her off her feet and detonated.

The blast slammed her body into the far wall with enough force to shatter the stone. She slid down the wall and started laughing as I approached. I saw the blood trickle out of the side of her mouth. She spat blood on the floor and traced a rune into the ground before I could rub it out with my boot.

"What did you do?" I felt the first tremor seconds later. She had detonated the runes above us.

"I killed you," she said with a smile. "This is going to be our grave, Night Warden Stryder. Now all of the Wardens will be together."

I ran to the door leading to the outer armory. Half of the level had collapsed and buried the bunk beds holding the rummers. It looked like the other half was about to come down any second. I ran back into the inner armory and my eyes fell on the vault.

I scooped up Lyrra and jumped into the vault, pulling the door closed behind us. Once the door closed, the circle activated and the world vanished.

FORTY-ONE

I OPENED MY eyes and found myself in a large bed. My first thought was Lyrra and the rummers. I sat up and a gentle but firm hand held me in place.

"You need rest, Grey." It was Aria. She wore her usual white robe covered in silver runic brocade, and it shone as it reflected the light of the morning sun. "No sudden movements."

"Lyrra... I had her in the circle." I looked around. "Wait, that circle led to The Cloisters?"

Aria gave me a look. "Try again."

"You intercepted a teleport?" I said, shocked. "How did you pull that off? According to Ziller's theorems of teleportation, that's supposed to be impossible."

"Not when you're wearing my runes."

"Your runes?" I said, not making the connection. "The duster?"

She nodded. "Ziller may be a member of the living library, but it doesn't mean he knows everything," she said. "Besides, he wasn't always the best student."

"Lyrra?"

"She barely made the jump." Aria shook her head slowly. "Her body had suffered too much trauma, and she had taken too much Redrum. Her mind was destroyed. She died shortly after arriving."

"I never found out who helped her make the new strain of Redrum."

"I was able to get a name—Haran," she said. "He was an Exile who left us several years ago." She gestured, and I heard footsteps. "You can pursue that when you recover."

"Wait, how did you know to even track my coat?"

She pointed to the door. Koda came in, carrying Frank.

"I told her," Frank said. He made a motion to spit and stopped himself after looking at Aria. "Lockpick over here was in a bad way, and I figured she was better off here, considering her condition."

"Did you at least tell Roxanne?"

"She was the one who worked on Lockpick, along with Ms. Aria."

I raised an eyebrow at his formality and nodded. "Smart dragon."

"I'm glad to see you're okay." Koda fidgeted for a few seconds. "Stryder?"

"Ask already."

"Do you have my fans?" she asked and blushed. "I would have waited to ask, but I feel so wrong without them. Please tell me you didn't leave them down there."

"In my coat," I growled at her. "I'll give them to you later. Fans, really?"

"Please allow Grey to get some rest." Aria motioned for them to leave the room. "You can visit again later."

"I'll let Cole know you're still kicking," Frank said as Koda carried him out. "Do you want me to tell Montague?"

"Hold off on that for a while."

Last thing I needed was a mage heart-to-heart. I knew as soon as Rox found out, he would be here to counsel me on the dangers of using the sword. I could wait a few days for that conversation.

"How long do I have to stay here?" I asked Aria after they had left. "This is much better than Haven, but I don't like hospitals—even magical ones."

"You bonded with the Izanami."

It wasn't a question.

"Didn't have much of a choice." I looked away. "Didn't expect to be coming back, either."

"But you have."

"I have no idea what I'm doing with this thing. Is it still in my coat?"

"Check closer." She pointed at my chest. "You can't be separated from it now. The spell attacking your body has been rendered inert."

I let my senses expand and there it was, resting inside of me. "Oh for fu"—Aria raised an eyebrow—"for fudge sake. This thing is inside me now?"

"I will give you instructions—if you promise to follow them," Aria said, looking at me and shaking her head. "I mean, *really* follow them."

"Fine, if it means I get out of here faster."

"It does." She walked to door and stopped. "I'm pleased you survived your ordeal, Grey."

"Me too," I said. "There were a few moments there where I wasn't sure."

"Get some rest." She gestured, the lights dimmed, and the curtains closed, blocking out the sun. The room was cast into a pleasant darkness. "You still have much work to do, Night Warden."

***

Several hours had passed, when a presence woke me. The sun had set, and the darkness that settled over my room now had an edge of menace.

"Did you find the source of the new strain of Redrum?" a voice said from the darkness—Hades.

"Yes and no." I sat up in bed, fully awake. "I still need to find the Exile who altered the Redrum."

"Clearly she didn't work out," he said. "Keep the sword as a token of my sincerity. I'll have her taken care of."

Like I could return it now—the bastard. I looked around and noticed Corbel was missing.

"No."

"No? To what exactly?"

"She stays with me." I couldn't see his face, but his presence filled the room. I saw him sitting in the corner, a shadow in the night.

"She's a burden—you said so yourself." He stood and glided over to the window. "I'll retire her and end her pitiful existence."

I clenched my fist and found the sword in my hand as I left the bed. I felt the power and let it flow through me.

<I am yours and you are mine. He cannot stand against us.>

"Come," I whispered.

Black energy erupted from the blade as the runes along its length burst with light. Tendrils of darkness impaled me, and I felt the power and consciousness of Izanami join with my own.

Hades crossed his arms behind his back.

"Do you think you're powerful enough to stop me?"

"Want to find out?"

"You wouldn't use it to save yourself, but you willingly surrender to it to save her?"

"I'm funny that way."

"Very well." He waved a hand in the air and sighed. "I will concede your request. She is released from my employ."

"No repercussions?"

"None. She officially works for—"

I raised an eyebrow.

"*With* you from this moment forward."

"Thank you."

"And I you." He turned and looked out the window. "This is a fantastic view," he said, before disappearing.

Once I was sure he was gone, I exhaled and slumped against the bed as the room swam around me. Koda materialized in the corner and nearly gave me a heart attack.

"What have I told you about sneaking around?" I absorbed the sword and lay down. Her masking had improved—not even Hades gave any indication he had sensed her. It was most likely Aria's doing. At this rate, I would never have any privacy.

"Thank you," she said softly.

I waved her off. "Don't thank me. Stop pissing me off and we can call it even."

"I'll be outside."

"You do that, and let me get some sleep," I snapped.

"Like I need guarding in The Cloisters. Give me a break."

She padded out of the room, and I caught my breath. Using the sword had taken me by surprise—I wasn't ready to use it yet. I had a lot to learn and teach. The Night Wardens I trained with were gone, but there was still a city to protect.

I let my senses expand and felt Koda sitting outside the room, vigilant. She was going to make an excellent Night Warden.

THE END

AUTHOR NOTES

THANK YOU FOR reading this story and jumping into the world of Grey Stryder and the Night Wardens. If you've read the Montague & Strong books, you will find things that are familiar and a few that are new.

This story started with the question: Who dealt with the fallout from Monty & Strong's activities? It turns out to be Grey Stryder and his group of friends, and he's usually not happy about it, but as the saying goes: it's a dirty job and someone has to do it.

This book (series) gives you a different perspective of the Monty & Strong world. It's grittier and darker and Grey is reluctant to take on the role of being hero. Along with Koda, they will find themselves in over their heads most of the time, facing enemies and situations with no easy solution. Like Montague & Strong, I want to introduce you to different elements of the world Grey & Koda inhabit, slowly revealing who they are and why they make the choices they do. I know there are many unanswered questions. I promise to address them all over time, with the full knowledge that the answers will only raise new questions.

There are references you may understand and some…you may not. This may be attributable to my age (I'm older than Grey too, or at least feel that way most mornings) or to my love of all things sci-fi and fantasy. As a reader, I've always enjoyed finding these "Easter Eggs" in the books I read. I hope you do too. If there is a reference you don't get, feel free to email me and I will explain it…maybe.

You will notice that Koda, for all her skill still seems naïve and uninformed about Grey's world. That will change as time passes. Be patient with her…she has a lot of learning to do, and doesn't trust anyone.

Each book will reveal more about Grey and Koda's backgrounds and lives before they met. Rather than hit you with a whole history, I wanted you to learn about them slowly, the way we do with a person we just met —over time (and many cups of Death Wish Coffee).

Thank you for taking the time to read this book. I wrote it for you and I hope you enjoyed spending a few hours getting in (and out of) trouble with Grey, Koda & company.

If you really enjoyed this story, I need you to do me a **HUGE** favor—**Please leave a review**.

It's important and helps the book (and me). In addition, it means Frank can keep The Dive safe from strangers without resorting to lethal electrical methods.

We want to keep Frank's cranky level down to a minimum, don't we?

I really do appreciate your feedback. Let me know what you thought by emailing me at:
www.orlando@orlandoasanchez.com

For more information on Monty & Strong…come
join the MoB on Facebook!
You can find us at:
Montague & Strong Case Files.
To get FREE books visit my page at:
www.orlandoasanchez.com

SPECIAL MENTIONS FOR WANDER:

MANDY J. PANTS: Because you asked the question: Why doesn't anyone have a thorny dragon as a magical pet?

Renee Smith-for aboriginal/Indigenous research on Frank's origins.

Dan F. because General Java and the Chinese calendar system for Street.

Noah S. The Character Quirk Master.

Jim Z. because Grey has Magisthesia-magical synesthesia.

Charlotte C. because you gave Jim the idea.

Dolly for Grey's NY Cheesecake fixation and ability to speak any language.

Denise K. for his love of stained glass windows and the Painkiller.

Larry for being truly sincastic. I hope the L3 pile implodes your Kindle in the nicest way possible.

Amanda & Heather H: Because I can't drink coffee around you two without the danger of projectile expulsion. Thank you for the laughter and just being you.

Larry & Jim Because we ALL need a Tushman-Ziller L3 Quantum Kindle titanium waterproof edition.

TAGLINES FOR THE DIVE-THIS NEEDS ITS OWN SECTION:

GREY S.:
THE Dive-Drink in peace or leave in pieces.

Mages, Mischief, and Madness-just take it outside.

Mandy J. Pants:
We do not meddle in the affair of dragons for we are crunchy and taste good with ketchup and interior decorations in The Dive.

If you find the food and drinks offensive we suggest you stop finding us.

Welcome to the Dive-please lower your standards.

Noah S.
Be discreet or be delicious.

If you could read, you wouldn't be here.

The Dive-not technically a death trap

Don't vomit on my stuff.

Probably not a front for organized crime.

Larry L3:
Because we never settle for the shallow end.

Ethanol!

Laura CR:

You have to go deep to drink in low places.

Check your weapons at the door.

The Dive-We're not your friends, but it's better than drinking alone.

Simon C:

Where no one knows your name or gives a toss.

John J:

The Dive-how low can you get.

Marie McC:

The Dive-good times-don't lose your head.

Corrine L:

Yes we serve food-just don't ask what's in it.

Mark M:

The Dive- We set our expectations low so you can meet them.

Mary M:

You get what you get or you get out.

Amanda S:

The Dive- We serve food, drinks, and undesirables.

We put the DIE in Dive.

Bernice L:

The Dive where the lights are low, the drinks strong, and the clientele wild.

Joscelyn S.

The Dive-Nowhere to go but up.

There are many more and will be added as the books continue…keep an eye out!

Thank You!

If you enjoyed this book, would you please help me by leaving a review at the site where you purchased it from? It only needs to be a sentence or two and it would really help me out a lot!

All of My Books

The Warriors of the Way
The Karashihan* • Spiritual Warriors • The Ascendants • The Fallen Warrior • The Warrior Ascendant • The Master Warrior

John Kane
The Deepest Cut* • Blur

Sepia Blue
The Last Dance* • Rise of the Night

Chronicles of the Modern Mystics
The Dark Flame • A Dream of Ashes

Montague & Strong Detective Agency
Tombyards & Butterflies• Full Moon Howl•Blood Is Thicker• Silver Clouds Dirty Sky • NoGod is Safe•The Date

Night Warden
Wander

*Books denoted with an asterisk are FREE via my website.
www.OrlandoASanchez.com

ACKNOWLEDGMENTS

I'm finally beginning to understand that each book, each creative expression usually has a large group of people behind it. This story is no different. So let me take a moment to acknowledge my (very large) group:

To Dolly: my wife and biggest fan. You make all of this possible and keep me grounded, especially when I get into my writing to the exclusion of everything else. Thank you, I love you.

To my Tribe: You are the reason I have stories to tell. You cannot possibly fathom how much and how deep I love you all.

To Lee: Because you were the first audience I ever had. I love you sis.

To the Logsdon family: JL your support always demands I bring my A-game and produce the best story I can. I always hear: "Don't rush!" in your voice.

L.L. (the Uber Jeditor) your notes and comments turned this story from good to great. I accept the challenge!

Your patience knows no bounds. Thank you both.

Arigatogozaimasu

<u>The Montague & Strong Case Files Group AKA- The MoB(The Mages of BadAssery)</u>

When I wrote T&B there were fifty-five members in The MoB. As of this writing there are 430 members in the MoB. I am honored to be able to call you my MoB Family. This story mostly came about because you kept asking for it. I hope you enjoy it.

Thank you for being part of this group

and M&S. You each make it possible.

THANK YOU.

<u>WTA-The Incorrigibles</u>

JL,BenZ, EricQK, S.S., and the Mac

They sound like a bunch of badass misfits because they are. Thank you for making sure I didn't rush this one. My exposure to the slightly deranged and extremely deviant brain trust that you are made this book possible. I humbly thank you and it's all your fault.

<u>To Gene Mollica Design</u>

Gene, Cristin, Paul, Jordan

You define professionalism and creativity. Thank you for the great service and amazing covers.

YOU GUYS RULE!

<u>To you the reader:</u>

Thank you for jumping down the rabbit hole with me. I truly hope you enjoy this story. You are the reason I wrote it.

ART SHREDDERS

No book is the work of just one person. I am fortunate enough to have an excellent team of readers and shredders who give of their time and keen eyes to provide notes, insight, and corrections. They help make this book go from good to great. Each and every one of you helped make this book fantastic.

THANK YOU

Amanda H. Amanda S. Amanda W. Amy R. Andrew G. Anita W. Audra V. M. Barbara H. Bennah P.

Beth M. Bill T. Brandon A. Brandy D. Brenda Nix L. Caroline L. Carrie Anne O. Cassandra H.

Charlotte C. Chris B. Claudia L-S.

Corrine L. Daniel P. Darla H. Darren M. Dawn G. Denise K.

Donald T. Heather H. Helen V. Jacce J. Jayne M. Jen C. Jennifer W. Joscelyn S. Joseph M. Julian M.

Julie Rogers H. Kandice S. Karen H. Kimbra S. Klaire T. Larry Diaz T. Laura Cadger R. Laura Maria R.

Lesley S. Leslie K. Linda M. Liz C. Mandy J.P. Marie McC. Mary M. MaryAnn S. Marydot H.P.

Matt-Eileen R. Melody DeL. Michelle S. Mike H. Natalie F. Noah S. Oddegeir O L. Robert J. Robert W.

Samantha L. Sara Mason B. Shannon O'B. Sharyn W. Stacey S. Stephanie C. Steve Woofie W. Sue W.

Susan B. Tami C. Tammy T. Terri A. Timothy L. Tommy O. Tracy B. Tracy K. Tracy M. Trish V. B.

William N.

ABOUT THE AUTHOR

Orlando Sanchez has been writing ever since his teens when he was immersed in creating scenarios for playing Dungeon and Dragons with his friends every weekend. An avid reader, his influences are too numerous to list here. Some of the most prominent are: J.R.R. Tolkien, Jim Butcher, Kat Richardson, Terry Pratchett, Christopher Moore,Terry Brooks, Piers Anthony, Lee Child, George Lucas, Andrew Vachss, and Barry Eisler to name a few in no particular order.

The worlds of his books are urban settings with a twist of the paranormal lurking just behind the scenes and generous doses of magic, martial arts, and mayhem.

Aside from writing, he holds a 2nd and 3rd Dan in two distinct styles of Karate. If not training, he is studying some aspect of the martial arts or martial arts philosophy.

He currently resides in Queens, NY with his wife and children and can often be found in the local Starbucks where most of his writing is done.

Please visit his site at OrlandoASanchez.com for more information about his books and upcoming releases.

Made in the USA
Monee, IL
29 April 2024